T0122014

# THE EYE
## OF THE
# GODDESS

---

Protector of the Crystal Children

---

Debbie Russell

**BALBOA.**
PRESS
A DIVISION OF HAY HOUSE

ISBN: 978-1-4525-5658-1 (sc)
ISBN: 978-1-4525-5657-4 (e)
ISBN: 978-1-4525-5656-7 (hc)

Library of Congress Control Number: 2012914136

Balboa Press books may be ordered through booksellers or by contacting:

Balboa Press
A Division of Hay House
1663 Liberty Drive
Bloomington, IN 47403
www.balboapress.com
1-(877) 407-4847

Printed in the United States of America

Balboa Press rev. date: 09/06/2012

# CONTENTS

# Acknowledgements

First off, I would like to thank my wonderful children, Mark and Jordan Iltchenko. Without their love and light, nothing else would be possible. They encourage me to do my best every day of my life.

❖ ❖ ❖

I would also like to acknowledge Pia Gabriela, my cover designer. She is beyond awesome! Her pictures always go above and beyond my wildest imagination!

❖ ❖ ❖

Thank you to Susan Romero, my first editor. She whipped me into shape as a beginning writer, and I really appreciate all the time and effort she put into my writing when I had no idea what I was doing!

❖ ❖ ❖

Doreen Virtue, Edgar Cayce and Masashi Kishimoto have been major influences on my writing. All three of these people are phenomenal. I am a better person after reading their works.

❖ ❖ ❖

To Tammy Sherer, my wonder twin: Thank you for being the best friend a person could ever want! And thank you for giving me the confidence to pursue my dreams.

❖ ❖ ❖

I would like to thank Laura West, Tina Marie Daly and Melissa Virtue. Laura was the one that suggested that I become a writer. I am eternally grateful for that. Then Tina Marie and Melissa encouraged me when I really wanted to give up. Thank you for being there for me when the chips were down.

❖ ❖ ❖

Lastly, I couldn't have finished this book without my beta-readers. Their encouragement and helpful hints have been invaluable. Catherine Berganza, Maria Naritsin, Leilani Zeller, Rachel Milburn, and Jeffrey Kaufman: you are my best of friends and I will never forget the help that you have given me.

❖ ❖ ❖

# CHAPTER ONE

## Jordan's Birthday

Something was after Jordan. She didn't know what, but she frantically looked around to try to find it. The problem was ... there was nothing but darkness. She could hear footsteps, and deep inside her gut she could feel that whatever was coming was definitely something she needed to avoid.

She could detect a faint light, and it illuminated her path enough that she realized she was in a maze. Where was she supposed to turn? Where was the light really coming from? She didn't have time to think about it. She couldn't just stand still. There was something in the darkness with her, and she didn't want to find out what it was. She had to keep moving forward, away from that presence.

She tried to run toward the light, but she stumbled and fell a couple of times along the way. Each time, as she got up, she cringed and tried to shield herself. She could almost feel an ice-cold hand wrap around her neck, and in the darkness, she couldn't tell if it was real or just her imagination. She was scratched, skinned, and battered. But she didn't give up. She was going to find a way out of the darkness no matter what. She turned the corner, and finally, she saw the way out. Straight ahead, the light seemed to be getting brighter. Triumphantly, she ran faster so she could finally break free. As she got closer, she shielded her eyes from the brightness. It was too intense in comparison to where she had come from.

As she emerged from the tunnel, she saw some familiar faces. However, the rest of their appearance seemed completely different. Her mother was standing there, her long, brown hair gently whipping in the wind that was circling them. But her mother's form was shrouded in a pearl-white glow.

Next to her mother was Jordan's dark-haired, sixteen-year-old brother. He smiled at Jordan and nodded in her direction, seeming to indicate that she was where she needed to be. He was also surrounded by the same colored aura.

She tried to scream, but no sound came out of her mouth. It seemed that wherever this place was, it was devoid of verbal communication. Feeling panicked, she gestured at the tunnel, desperate to tell them about the approaching danger. She turned back to them, her body shaking, and tried to motion for them to run away. She didn't want to get caught by whatever was after her, and she certainly didn't want it to get her family either. She wanted them to run and to take her with them.

But strangely, instead of heeding her unspoken warning, her mother and brother simply stepped aside. In their place appeared a handsome, tall, blond-haired man. Well, maybe not a man, but an older teenage boy that seemed to be about the same age as her older brother. Again, he had the same pearl-white aura that her family had. Jordan looked down at herself, and she had the same aura all over her as well. What kind of place was this that everyone seemed to be glowing?

The blond boy gestured an open hand toward her, and she just looked at it for a minute. A warm smile crossed his face, as if he was trying to say that he wouldn't harm her. However, she still did not accept his hand.

*Who is he and where did he come from? Why should I trust him? Maybe he's the one I've been running from.* She looked back toward the tunnel. The scary presence might still come out of it at any second. Noticing her concern, the boy looked toward the tunnel, and with a simple wave of his hand, the tunnel sealed up. Then, before her eyes, the entire dark-red rock formation from where she had emerged disappeared into thin air.

She turned toward the mysterious boy again. *How does he have the power to do that? And did he really just get rid of whoever or whatever was following me?*

The older blond boy walked up and gently put his arm around her shoulder. She suspiciously looked at the arm that was touching her and reluctantly followed him away from her original spot. In front of her, she could see a huge crowd of other glowing children standing in the middle of a rolling green meadow. Each of these children had striking, radiant eyes. Jordan was taken aback by this at first. She had large, crystal blue eyes, which were unusual compared to most people she met. But the eyes of these children all seemed to match.

She looked up at the young man standing beside her. He had large, dark blue eyes. When he looked down to gaze directly at her, she could see herself in his eyes—both her physical reflection and her scared, inner child. It unnerved her, so she stepped away from his grasp.

The young man then motioned for Jordan to turn, and when she did, she saw a woman with enormous wings. She was standing at the other side of a creek that seemed to divide the green meadow. The woman was surrounded by a shimmering, cerulean blue light. From behind her, a large cerulean blue dragon started to take flight. The dragon looked down at the woman and blew a puff of smoke, as if he was initiating a conversation with her. In response, the woman jumped on the dragon's back, and both of them flew away toward the horizon.

As Jordan watched them, she thought to herself that the two seemed to belong with each other. The woman's aura completely matched the color of the dragon, and both had similar wings. The only difference was that the dragon's wings were flat and smooth, and the woman's wings were more feather-like and multi-layered. But both beings seemed to have a symbiotic relationship. The cerulean blue aura that surrounded them became more intense as they joined together.

It was interesting. Everyone else was glowing pearl-white. How did those two have a different colored aura than everyone else? What was up with those two?

Jordan reviewed her immediate surroundings again. All the eyes of her family, the blond young man, and the angelic looking children were staring at her. They appeared to be waiting for her instructions. Jordan froze at the thought. What was she supposed to do now? She started to sweat and get nervous. Maybe the woman with the cerulean blue aura would know what to do. Why did she have to leave so suddenly?

The anticipation on the young kids' faces was heartbreaking. They were waiting for orders that would never come. Jordan instinctively knew that each and every one of those children would follow her wherever she might go, and she started to feel sick about it. She had no idea where she was going, so she certainly didn't want to feel responsible for getting them lost as well.

*Where is this place and who are these people? They're all assembled like miniature soldiers getting ready for battle.*

*Is this my army? And what are we supposed to be fighting for? What kind of army is comprised of young children and led by a thirteen-year-old? Why are all these people staring at me like I have all the answers? I'm not about to lead them anywhere. Why don't they stare at the blond guy? He seems pretty strong, and he's older than I am.*

The crowd of pearl-white glowing beings started stepping closer to her. Jordan didn't know what to do, and the panic she felt from the tunnel was back. But this time, the fear was different. This time, she was afraid that she would fail all of these people that seemed to depend on her. This led to a desperation that caused her to stop breathing, and she was seized by a drowning sensation. She felt her knees buckle, and she started to fall to the ground.

But before her head could hit the grass-covered earth, Jordan was wrenched out of the dream. She felt sweat dripping down her face, so she wiped her brow.

*What a weird dream! What did she eat last night to bring that on?*

Jordan Ivanov slowly got up out of her bed and walked toward the mirror. A young, scared girl stared back at her.

*At least the pearl-white aura is gone! Why did I have a dream about a bunch of people that I don't even know who evidently wanted me to lead them?*

Jordan was relatively weak in her own opinion. Her enormous, crystal blue eyes started to survey what they saw in the mirror. Physically, she saw a slight, young girl. Jordan was on the shorter side, being around five feet tall. She was thin, and fair to the point that she almost seemed translucent. Her strawberry-blonde hair was straight and long, reaching all the way down to her waist.

Jordan shook her head and tried to snap herself back to reality. She had to get ready. Today was her thirteenth birthday, and her family was heading to SeaWorld in Orlando. They lived in Tampa, Florida, so the drive would take only a couple of hours. Since it was Saturday, they had decided to make a day of it and spend the night in a hotel before returning home.

By the time Jordan made it to the breakfast table, everyone was already eating. Her mother was perched at the kitchen counter, as usual. Even though she was forty-five years old, she still looked young and beautiful. As the rest of them ate, her mother rushed around and made sure all of the family's needs were met. All the while, her food got cold. Her mother would end up finishing her meal while she washed the dishes.

Jordan's mom, Catherine, had spent her whole life taking care of others. Her own mother had died of diabetes when Catherine was only nineteen. But before that, her time as a teenager had been spent tending to her dying mother. In Jordan's mind, Catherine was the most unselfish person she ever met. It was almost as if she was born that way and never knew that there was any other way to be.

People would tell Jordan that she resembled her mother, but Jordan didn't see it. Both wore their hair long, but Catherine's was thick and brown, whereas Jordan's was thin and strawberry blonde. Catherine was fair-skinned, but she was nowhere near as fair as Jordan. Catherine had brown eyes, which could not compare to Jordan's crystal blue orbs. And her mother was slim and six inches taller than Jordan, who was downright skinny.

Jordan took her place at the circular table next to her brother. They always sat side by side while eating their meals. Jordan and her brother, Mark, had never had a typical sibling relationship. Jordan remembered a story about her brother and how he acted when they first brought newborn Jordan home from the hospital. Catherine awoke one night to find three-year-old Mark standing guard outside of Jordan's bedroom door. He was wearing his ninja costume from Halloween and was armed with a plastic sword. When Catherine asked Mark what he was doing, he told her that he was protecting his sister from the monsters that were after her.

Mark's instinct to protect his sister only grew over time. As a result, they were always together. Mark wanted to protect her, and Jordan found that she wanted to be protected. But there was a downside also. Being around each other all the time led to a love/hate relationship. They were either the best of friends, or they would fight all the time. It really depended on their mood on any given day.

Jordan always felt shy around people, but she thought Mark was more distant than shy. Nevertheless, everyone was drawn to him. At sixteen years old, he was five foot ten, well-built, athletic, and very handsome. Mark preferred to keep his straight, dark brown hair medium length, with the sides cut to reveal half of his ears and the back just long enough to reach his shoulders. When he smiled, his warm hazel eyes sparkled. Mark had a darker complexion than Jordan, and he had a dimple on his right cheek that appeared when he smiled.

Jordan glanced to her other side, where her father sat at the table. He was an older version of Mark. Her father, Victor, had darker hair and a darker complexion than Mark, and his eyes were a darker shade of blue than Jordan's. Victor had served in the Soviet military, and he had maintained his muscular build from those days.

Victor handed Jordan a black velvet box.

"Happy birthday, sweetheart. Sorry about the trip."

Jordan smiled and took the box.

Victor returned her smile. "Does this mean you've forgiven me?"

"Of course." She couldn't stay mad at him. She knew he would have gotten out of his business trip if he could have.

Jordan opened the box and saw a white gold amulet inside. On it was etched a beautiful goddess holding up a shining orb above her head. Wrapped around the backside of the goddess was a majestic looking dragon.

*A goddess and a dragon? That's mighty familiar.*

"It's beautiful, Dad."

"This is actually a gift from your Great-Grandmother Ivanov. She wanted you to have it on your thirteenth birthday."

This bewildered Jordan. "But she died when you were a little boy."

Victor smiled. "It was passed down through the generations. It was her dying wish to keep this in the family."

Jordan took the amulet out of the box. She held it up so that she could take a better look at it. Then, in her mind's eye, the goddess and dragon came to life. They were the same ones from her dream, but this time, the goddess did not have wings. Both of them glowed with their cerulean blue aura. In this vision, they were not in a green meadow but were surrounded by a starry sky. The goddess was holding a sparkling yellow globe above her head, and the dragon was obediently stationed behind her, seemingly on standby to protect her if necessary.

"Are you all right?" Her mother's voice startled Jordan out of her reverie. Jordan shook her head and blinked a few times. Then she took another look at the white gold amulet. *That's them! The goddess and dragon in my dream exactly match the figures on this necklace. What's this supposed to mean?*

Victor looked at his daughter with a hurt expression on his face. "You don't like it, do you?"

"No! Dad, it's not that." How could she explain to him how she really felt?

Jordan looked around at each of her family members, who were staring back at her expectantly. She couldn't avoid it, so she slowly unclasped the necklace. She took a deep breath before wrapping it around her neck.

# Chapter Two

## Trip to Orlando

*A*s Jordan climbed into the backseat of the car for her big trip, she tried to not think about her necklace. They were headed toward the hotel to drop off their luggage, and then they would go to SeaWorld.

Right before they drove into the hotel parking lot, they passed a metaphysical shop named Crystals and Mystical Gifts. After Catherine parked the car, she turned around and asked, "Can we stop by there on the way back?"

Catherine always had an interest in the metaphysical, so the request did not surprise her children. From the backseat, Jordan and Mark gave each other the *here we go again* look and then shrugged their shoulders in unison, letting Catherine know it was fine with them. At times, the family's non-verbal cues were even stronger than their verbal communication.

The trip to SeaWorld went well. The whole family loved dolphins, and the other sea animals were fun to watch as well. But Catherine couldn't stop talking about the metaphysical store. Since Jordan received her amulet that morning, her mother wanted to find a book that talked about amulets. Catherine wanted to see what kind of connection the necklace would bring between Jordan and her great-grandmother.

After having dinner at the park, they headed back to the hotel and stopped at the crystal store. As they stepped through the doorway, Jordan noticed that it was decorated with oriental rugs, chandeliers, and crystal balls, reminding her of accessories used by gypsies from olden times. The smell of burning incense floated in the air, and relaxing music played in the background.

Catherine marveled at the array of crystals, candles, and incense and then stopped to look through the titles of the New Age literature. That's when the store owner approached her. The store owner was tall and slim with black, straight, thick hair that extended all the way down her back. She wore a gold crown across her forehead, which had a ruby in the center. The oval stone was about two inches from top to bottom. Her eyes were black and dark as night. In contrast, her skin was pale as a ghost. For a woman, she showed no softness at all. She had a long, narrow face and did not smile. She wore a form-fitting black dress that covered her down to her ankles.

"Hello. My name is Megaera." Her voice was deep for a female, and her tone was confident and authoritative.

Jordan saw her mother tense up as the store owner stood beside her. But her mother was always very polite. "It's nice to meet you. My name is Catherine."

Jordan's mom took a good look at Megaera and then asked, "Do I know you? You look familiar."

"I don't think so," Megaera purred.

Megaera turned her head to look at Mark. He immediately backed away from her. It was plain to see that the woman gave Mark the creeps.

At that point, Megaera fixed her gaze on Jordan. It didn't look like she was going to let Jordan get away like Mark did. She slowly walked toward Jordan, as her black eyes flashed, and she extended her hand to the young girl. Jordan looked at the outstretched hand for a second, trying to decide what to do.

The woman creeped Jordan out. Jordan longed to pull back like her brother had, but she had better manners. It just wouldn't be polite. Still, those black eyes made ice crawl up Jordan's spine.

She finally reached over and shook Megaera's hand.

Megaera jerked as if she had been struck by an electrical jolt. She immediately withdrew her hand and stared incredulously at Jordan. Jordan, for her part, was completely freaked out.

*She is mega-weird. If that dress and crown wasn't freaky enough, then her actions would definitely call her out.*

Megaera's eyes flashed again as she noticed Jordan's amulet around her neck.

"That is a beautiful piece of jewelry. Do you know what the symbols on it mean?" Megaera asked.

"No, I just got the necklace today."

"Well, the goddess symbolizes protection, while the dragon signifies strength. As long as you wear the amulet, you will always be strong and protected."

Megaera pulled the amulet in for a closer look. Jordan felt the chain tighten around her neck. She could still breathe but just barely. She made a coughing noise to let the woman know, but Megaera paid it no attention.

Megaera pointed to the etching on the amulet and said, "Furthermore, the goddess is holding an illuminated orb above her. That symbolizes that with the help of your goddess and dragon, you will have the world in your hands."

At long last, the woman released the amulet. Jordan gulped a lungful of air. She didn't know if she imagined it, but it felt like Megaera was trying to choke Jordan with her own necklace!

"Do you have any books that talk about amulets?" Catherine asked from across the room.

In a huff, Megaera treaded over to Catherine, and without any thought, pulled out exactly the book that Catherine wanted.

"How did you do that? I have been looking back and forth through that stack."

Megaera sneered, "It wasn't difficult."

If Jordan's mom noticed Megaera's weird demeanor, then she obviously chose to ignore it. She wrote out a check and paid Megaera for the book. Immediately, the three family members left the shop.

❋ ❋ ❋

As soon as they were gone, Megaera walked toward the back room of the shop. She reached for the door knob, and it slowly creaked open. On the other side, a young, blond man sat facing the wall. At the sound of the opening door, he turned around to face Megaera. His dark blue eyes had an irritated look to them.

"She's ready. Here is their address. Pay them a visit on Monday." Megaera handed Catherine's check to the young man. He stood up, and being a couple of inches taller than Megaera, he looked down into her piercing eyes.

"What do you expect me to do when I get there?"

If Megaera could smile, she would have. But since it would most likely break her face, she just smirked at the blond boy. "You'll figure something out."

❋ ❋ ❋

It had been a long, eventful day. When the three of them got to their hotel room, all of them got ready for bed. The room had two queen-sized beds and a pull-out couch. Jordan chose the bed by the window. Her brother settled for the bed next to hers, and her mother got the couch ready. As soon as the light was out, everyone fell sound asleep.

In the middle of the night, Jordan started to toss and turn. She felt a strong energy that seemed to resonate with the amulet she was wearing. She opened her eyes and noticed a bright light in the room.

It was a pearl-white glow, just like the one in her dream. The glow permeated the room. It flowed through the window, under the door, and from the light fixtures. It got brighter and brighter until, in the middle of the room, the goddess appeared with her cerulean blue aura. She opened her wings, and they spanned seven feet across.

The goddess was just like Jordan remembered her. *Am I still dreaming? This must be a dream!*

She looked lovingly at Jordan as she floated toward her. Then she knelt down at Jordan's bedside.

"Who … who are you?" Jordan stuttered.

Her voice was soft and gentle, like a young child's whisper, yet loud enough for Jordan to hear. "I am Theia. Don't you recognize me?"

"No, not really."

"I guess that's not surprising. But I've been waiting for you."

Jordan looked directly at Theia with a stunned expression. "Why? Why would you be waiting for me?"

"Because you have a lot to do in this lifetime."

*Oh hell. Don't tell me that dream was for real.* "What do I need to do?"

Theia gently smiled. "You need to lead the Crystal Children in transforming this planet into the peaceful place that God had always intended."

*What the what? She has to be kidding!* Jordan looked down and didn't know what to say.

Theia chuckled. "You know that I can read your thoughts, right? You can't really keep things from me."

*Okay. That's a bit inconvenient.* "What's a Crystal Child?"

"They are incarnated angels that have powers similar to yours."

"Similar to mine? I don't have any powers!"

Theia giggled. "Yes you do. You just haven't used them yet."

"Um ... I'm pretty sure that I would've noticed if I had any type of powers. That is kinda hard to miss."

Unfazed, Theia just smiled at Jordan. "Very well then. Let me unlock those for you."

The goddess took her hands and placed them above Jordan's stomach, and a vortex of white light appeared. Jordan watched with amazement as the vortex entered her body, and she started to glow pearl white. Inside of her, she started to feel warm all over like she was immersed in a hot bath on a winter morning.

Then the goddess placed her hands directly on Jordan's shoulders until the pearl-white glow that surrounded Jordan turned cerulean blue. With this energy change, it felt more like an electrical current than a calming sensation, but it wasn't altogether unpleasant.

Theia lifted her hands away from Jordan, and the aura returned back to her natural color.

"How does that feel?" Theia asked in her normal whisper.

"Weird. What did you do?"

"You will see in due time. I am going to do something similar to your mother and brother. You will need their help in the future."

Jordan watched from her bedside as Theia floated to Mark. She waved her hand over him and released cerulean blue sparkles that covered him from head to toe. He glowed pearl white for a second and then returned to his normal color.

When Theia was done with Mark, she floated over to Catherine on the couch. She repeated the process. Jordan was amazed that neither one even stirred as all of this was happening.

Theia then turned back to Jordan. "I have to go now. I will see you soon."

"No, wait! What am I supposed to do now?"

"When you're needed, you will know."

"You think I can sleep after this? I'm going to wake them up and freak out!"

Theia laughed. "No you won't."

Theia floated back to Jordan and placed her hand over Jordan's eyelids. She gently closed them and then placed her arms and wings around Jordan. With Theia's wings cradling her body, the calming sensation took over. In a matter of seconds, Jordan fell back into a deep sleep.

# CHAPTER THREE

# The Law of Attraction

*T*here were thousands of them. They were all glowing pearl white, and their sparkling, crystal blue eyes were staring holes into her. Where was Theia? How could she leave her like this?

The light started to get brighter and more yellow in color. Then she felt someone tap her shoulder.

"Honey, it's time to wake up. We need to get ready to go back home," her mother whispered.

*Go back home!* Now she was awake. Jordan remembered what had happened the night before.

"Mom, a woman visited us last night! I think she was the goddess from my necklace." Jordan grabbed the amulet and pointed it toward her mother.

Catherine gently placed her hand over Jordan's and motioned for her daughter to lower the necklace. "Sounds like an interesting dream."

"Mom, it was real! She was really here!"

"I'm sure it felt that way."

"Goddesses usually don't visit people's hotel rooms in the middle of the night," Mark teased.

*Like you would know?* Jordan thought as she smiled back at him.

"I know more than you," Mark retorted.

Catherine's eyes opened wide. "Her lips didn't move."

"What do you mean?" Mark asked.

Catherine shook her head. "I was looking right at her. She didn't say a thing."

"But I heard her!"

"I heard her too. But she didn't *say* it."

Jordan looked down at her hands. *Oh hell. It's starting. Are these the powers that Theia was talking about?*

Catherine started to look concerned. "What else did Theia say?"

"Why do you care? You told me it was a dream!"

Catherine smiled at her daughter. "I'm sorry for doubting you. Please tell me more about this goddess."

Jordan gave a perturbed look to her mother, and then she turned and intentionally gave the same look to Mark. "She said that I was going to lead a bunch of angel children in transforming Earth into a peaceful place."

Mark tried to choke back his laughter. "You? Now I know it was a dream …"

Jordan wanted to see if it would work. *If it was up to you, then you would just lead us all off a cliff!*

"No. Just you," Mark grumbled.

Catherine looked at her two kids and then said, "Okay. This is getting serious. You mentioned powers. Well, what powers was this goddess talking about?"

"She wouldn't tell me!" Jordan was starting to feel frustrated. She got up off her bed, walked toward the dresser mirror, and reached for her hairbrush. But instead, as her hand lowered, the brush flew up to her hand.

She held the brush, looked at it, and turned toward her mother. "Did you see that?"

Catherine couldn't even talk. She just nodded.

"Oh crap. How did you do that?" Mark asked.

Jordan was having trouble breathing. She stood there for a minute, leaning against the dresser for support. Catherine approached her and tried to help, but Jordan shrugged her off.

After Jordan composed herself, she decided to go to the bathroom. She wanted to be alone with her thoughts. As she approached the door, she reached for the knob, and the door swung in her direction. Jordan was really frustrated now. *These powers really should come with some sort of manual. The next time I see Theia, I will give her a piece of my mind!* Jordan grabbed the door knob and slammed the door shut behind her.

On the car ride home, her mother tried to talk to her, but Jordan was no longer in a talking mood. Besides, Jordan could now read her mother's thoughts. Her mother did not want to upset her any further, especially since she could now send objects flying if she got really mad. Jordan chuckled at that last thought.

*That actually might make me feel better. I should try that when I get home.*

In response, Catherine glared at her through the rearview mirror.

When they got home, Catherine offered to fix lunch. Mark was hungry, but Jordan went straight to her room. She still didn't want to talk, and she knew that was the whole point of the meal.

Jordan climbed the stairs and headed straight to her room. She looked at the door, and in response, it closed at her unspoken command. *Hmm ... I guess that could be convenient.*

She flopped on her bed and looked out the window. Maybe being alone wasn't such a good idea after all.

*So what now?*

It was pretty lonely being surrounded by the four walls of her room. Even fighting with Mark would be better than a full day of solitude.

As she stared at the window, raindrops slowly fell from the sky. It made Jordan sad because it almost felt like the sky was crying for her. That was the last straw. Something was going to feel the brunt of her frustration, and now she knew what it was.

Jordan rolled off her bed, marched up to her window, wrenched it open, and screamed, "Enough is enough! Stop raining already! I can't take this too! I need a little sun in my life right now!"

Jordan stuck her head out of the window. Maybe the rain would magically wash away everything that had happened. She closed her eyes and waited to get wet. But it didn't happen. Instead, the raindrops stopped coming down. Jordan looked up and watched as the clouds suddenly disappeared, and the sun came out with all its brilliance.

"Are you going to jump out the window?" Mark asked.

Jordan hit her head against the top of the window at the realization that her brother was standing at her doorway. She turned around, rubbed her head, and gave him a deathly glare.

"With you as a brother, who could blame me?"

Catherine walked around Mark to enter Jordan's room. "Why were you yelling?"

Jordan shook her head. "Never mind that. Mom, it was just raining, and then it stopped. What do you think about that?"

Catherine gave her a confused look. "What am I supposed to think about that?"

"I told it to stop raining, and it did."

Catherine sighed. "Well, there is such a thing as atmokinesis, but maybe it was just a coincidence."

"Seriously? You think it's a coincidence with everything else that happened to us?" Jordan questioned.

"Happened ... *to you!*" Mark pointed out.

"Well Jordan, if you truly believe that you can manipulate the weather, why don't you show us and make it rain again?" Catherine asked.

"Hmpf." Jordan placed her hands on her hips defiantly. She swaggered over to the window, pointed to the sky, and said, "I want it to rain—*now!*"

She looked up to the sky for a few seconds, but nothing happened. Jordan was almost disappointed that she was wrong. But then a downpour came on suddenly and was so intense that her head got soaked, and she had to slam her window shut to avoid her whole room getting drenched.

She faced her mother and brother with a wide-eyed expression. They were pretty stunned. *Damn, that worked too well. I had better be careful what I say from now on.*

There was silence, and it was pretty unbearable. Then her mom said, "Come on, honey, let's get you dried off."

Catherine walked over, wrapped her arm around Jordan's shoulder, and led her to the bathroom to get a towel.

Mark looked at Jordan and then at her closed window. All the while, he was visibly trying to process everything in his mind.

The rest of the day and night, the three of them were verbally quiet with one another. But since they could read one another's thoughts, inside their minds it sounded like a never-ending traffic jam of rambling blabber. It was giving Jordan a headache, so she took some aspirin and went to bed rather early that night.

In her dreams, Jordan desperately tried to sort the whole thing out. *What does all this mean? Where are all the angel children?*

Jordan fixated on a different thought. *Who was the blond guy in my dream? I haven't seen him. Also, where is the dragon that I saw with Theia? And where does he fit into all of this?*

In her dream, the eyes were staring at her again. All of those magical looking eyes ... and they all seemed to see right through her. *Well, if my mother and brother can now read my mind, is it so surprising that these beings can see right through me? But then again, I don't think I like that! I don't like the idea of being totally exposed all the time. It's like walking around completely naked and pretending not to care! How did I get myself into this—and how do I get myself out?*

Jordan tossed and turned, and tossed and turned, and finally she got it! *I'm going to take off this freakin' necklace! Then maybe I can get back to my normal life!*

Jordan sat up and reached back to try to find the clasp, but then a hand cupped itself over hers to stop her.

With a loud gasp, Jordan twirled around to see Theia standing beside her. She appeared instantly and without warning. There she was with her cerulean blue aura and gigantic wings pulled together behind her back.

"You're going to need that."

"Hmpf. Is that so?"

Theia smiled. "But then again, maybe you don't. You have everything you need without it. The only thing the necklace gives you is a clear connection to me."

"And why would I want that?"

Theia gently laughed. "Why wouldn't you?"

"Because I want a normal life!"

"Too late."

*Grrr ... She's getting on my nerves!*

"Sorry." Theia giggled.

"Why do you like tormenting me?"

"I don't."

"Then why? Why are you doing this to me?"

Theia gave Jordan a confused look. "But we've been planning this since we met in Atlantis. This is something that you've wanted to do from the very beginning."

"Do what ... exactly?"

"Save the world, of course!"

*Yikes! That's it! If they have a home for crazy goddesses, then this particular one really needs to go there!*

At that, Theia outright laughed. "You think *I'm* crazy? You have no recollection of your past. How crazy is that?"

"Okay. Well, how about this? How about you fly away on that dragon of yours and leave me alone?"

"You mean Mael? You miss him, don't you? Well, don't worry. You'll see him soon. He can't exactly fit in the little rooms that you sleep in."

"Mael? What kind of name is that?"

"His name."

"Well, that clears it up."

"I knew it would."

"And I *don't* remember him, except for my dream. But that reminds me, how come your wings aren't on my necklace?"

"Because I was initiated into the heavens after I saved you and your family in Atlantis. But the necklace was forged when we met. I always wanted you to have a way to reach me."

"What did we need to be saved from?"

"Unfortunately, you'll see very soon. But for now, I had better go so that you can get some rest."

"Wait! You can't leave it like that!"

"I just did. Bye." Theia smiled as she casually waved and dematerialized from Jordan's room.

*Freakin' goddess just materializes in and out as she pleases. Who does she think she is?* But then Theia's gentle laugh echoed in her mind. *You're never really gone, are you?*

Jordan didn't even need a response. The feeling that helped her sleep in the hotel room was present again. And before she could even argue, she was sound asleep.

❀ ❀ ❀

The alarm clock on her nightstand went off at 8:00 a.m. Jordan groggily reached over to slam the offensive thing off. She looked around, and thank God, no heavenly messengers seemed to be hanging around at the moment. She swung her legs off the side of her bed, stretched her arms, and reluctantly got up.

Mark and Jordan were homeschooled, so it wasn't like she had to get dressed up in the morning. But, they did like to eat breakfast before starting their day at 9 a.m.

At 8:30, Jordan descended the staircase and headed toward the kitchen. Mark and Catherine looked up as she came in.

"What would you like to eat?" Catherine asked.

"French toast sticks," Jordan answered.

Mark diverted his attention from his bowl of cereal to ask, "Anything weird happen last night?"

"The goddess paid me another visit."

Mark grumbled, "She seems to really like you."

"Maybe I'll send her to your room next time."

"Please don't."

In the middle of their conversation, the doorbell rang. Catherine looked toward the doorway and then gave her children a questioning glance.

"I'm not expecting anyone," Mark blurted out.

"I'm not either. Who rings the doorbell at 8:30 in the morning?" Jordan asked.

"Only one way to find out," Mark said as he pushed back his chair and got up to see who it was. Jordan was curious, so she followed close behind him.

Mark opened their front door, and there he was—the blond guy from Jordan's dream! But he was much hotter in real life. He was leaning with his right arm against the door frame, but even so, Jordan could tell that he was a couple of inches taller than her brother. He looked like he was approximately the same age as Mark, but he had more of a confident air about him, bordering on arrogance. He had a slender build, but it appeared that every pound of his body was pure muscle. His golden blond hair was medium length and spiked at the top of his head.

Then she noticed his eyes. They were a deep, rich blue, like the depths of the ocean. They were so dark blue that it was a stark contrast to his light hair. His skin color was a medium-toned tan, which seemed to come as a result of working outdoors. And then his face ... it was adorable. And those lips ...

*Will you knock it off already!* Mark glared at his sister.

*Oh great! Now I can't even look at a guy without you butting in?* Jordan glared right back.

*Sickening* ... Mark faced the guy standing at the front door, who was now looking a tad impatient. "Can I help you?"

The young man replied in a deep, gravelly voice, "May I speak to the lady of the house?"

"Whatever for?" Mark asked, but then he got elbowed in the gut by Jordan.

"Right this way," Jordan said as she motioned him inside the doorway. Jordan followed him to the kitchen and took in the rest of his appearance. He was wearing a black tank top that exposed his broad, muscular shoulders. The shoulders were so broad that they seemed mismatched for his slimmer frame. Then she noticed his biceps and the rest of his physique. He looked like he had been training for the Olympics his whole life. She noticed his toned body, right down to his thighs, which appeared to be built to aptly sustain the weight of his torso ...

*You are making me physically ill.* Mark glared at his sister as he interrupted her train of thought.

*Good, that makes me want to do it even more!*

Jordan went to stare at the guy's butt, but then he turned around! He looked at her curiously, and in response, she turned away and blushed.

Mark laughed. *Serves you right.*

The mysterious young man walked up to Catherine. He stood there for a moment with his left hand in the pocket of his black cargo pants and his right hand holding onto an old, black backpack. He then steadied his look upon the matriarch of the family.

Catherine looked uncomfortable. She cleared her throat and asked, "Are you here to see someone?"

"You," he announced.

"Me? What is this about?"

"My guardian sent me here."

"To do what?"

"To study." The young man reached into his backpack and pulled out some papers.

Catherine reviewed the documents briefly and then looked back at the young man. "I don't understand."

"You have a teacher's certificate, right?"

Catherine was still confused, but she nodded her head.

"Well, I need someone to teach me."

"Why?"

The young man looked down at the floor. "I can't go to public schools."

Catherine was getting frustrated. "Why?"

"Because I was expelled."

Silence filled the room. Jordan didn't know why, but suddenly he became even more fascinating.

Mark broke the silence. "Why in the world would you think that my mom would be willing to teach you if you've been expelled? She doesn't need that type of problem, and neither do we."

The young man reached into his pocket and pulled out a check. "My guardian thought that she could use the money."

He handed the check to Catherine, and she looked at it. Her eyes bugged out. She didn't move, so Jordan and Mark walked around her to see what was wrong ... or maybe ... what was right. The check was for $50,000.

"Now, she was thinking that I could stay with you while I study this semester. We live far away from here."

Catherine didn't hear him. She was still looking at the check. But Jordan did, and she didn't know how to react. *How does one respond to the fact that a totally hot guy will be living with you? That's either really good or very, very bad.*

"Mom, why haven't you gotten rid of him yet? How do we know he isn't a total weirdo?" Mark asked as he looked at his mother.

Catherine stood there for a minute. She shifted her weight from one foot to the other. But then, Catherine shakily handed the young man the check. "I'm sorry. My son's right. I don't know you, and we don't usually invite total strangers to come live with us."

The young man hung his head and said, "I understand. It was a long shot. But I didn't really have a choice. I want to graduate by year-end so that I can go to college."

He walked back toward the front door, but then Jordan screamed, "Wait!"

He turned his head and quirked up his eyebrow at the young girl as she approached him.

"Let me talk to them. Wait here, okay?" Then she left him at the doorway.

She ran back to Catherine and Mark and said, "I think I know him."

Mark sneered, "You *wish* you knew him."

Jordan waved her hands in front of her face. "Forget that for a second." Jordan paused and pinched the bridge of her nose. "I had a dream before everything started happening to us. And *he* was in it. *He* was the remaining piece of the puzzle."

Jordan looked at her two family members and said, "Please. Please let him stay. Just long enough for me to figure out why he was in my dream. Please …"

Mark wasn't convinced, but Catherine sighed. "We'll let him stay one night. That's it. If things go well, then we'll take it from there. If they don't, then out he goes."

"That sounds more than fair. Thanks, Mom!"

"But he stays in Mark's room. That way he can keep an eye on him."

Mark gave a very evil laugh. Jordan hoped that the young man would survive the night without being suffocated by a pillow in his sleep.

Catherine walked out of the kitchen and toward the young man at the doorway. She looked up at him and asked, "What's your name?"

"Cole Morgan."

"Why did you get expelled?"

"Well, I've always been a little different than my classmates."

Jordan thought about that for a second and then asked, "Did you ever make the school disappear?"

"Um ... no."

*Lunatic.* Mark gave Jordan a pointed look.

*Mark, I swear! Can you please keep your thoughts to yourself for just a minute? I'm trying to figure out his connection to the dream!* Jordan looked over at her brother, and if looks could kill, he would have dropped dead right there.

"How does being different get you expelled?" Mark asked. He wasn't going to just let it go.

"My classmates were afraid of me. So to keep the peace, the school administrators thought this would be the easiest way."

"Did you do anything to *make* them afraid of you?"

In his gruff voice, Cole responded, "Not to my knowledge."

Catherine asked, "Maybe I should call your principal and find out?"

He turned to her with one eyebrow raised. "Aren't student records confidential?"

Unfazed, Catherine answered, "Not when the student is transferring to another school."

He shrugged. "Go ahead. I doubt he would remember me anyway."

*Huh? How could a principal not remember a student he expelled?* Jordan glanced briefly at her mother and brother. From the looks on their faces, they weren't buying it either.

Catherine stood there and looked Cole up and down. Jordan could only imagine her mother's thoughts, but she couldn't hear them.

"Cole, if you were planning to stay here, then is everything you need in that backpack?" Catherine asked.

Cole shook his head. "The rest of my stuff is in the car." He opened the door. A brand-new, red corvette was sitting in the driveway. If the $50,000 check didn't signal that he was from a rich family, well, the car just did.

Cole walked out and opened up the driver's side door. He folded up the front seat and grabbed a duffle bag from the back. Then without moving the front seat back to its normal position, he nudged the door closed with his right elbow.

As Cole approached the Ivanovs' front door, Mark sneered at him, "Is that where you keep the dead body?"

"I don't know. Why don't you check it just in case?" Cole suddenly tossed the bag at Mark, and since he wasn't expecting it, the bag knocked him to the ground.

"I hope there wasn't anything fragile in there," Catherine said from inside the doorway. *I would kind of like to know what he has in that bag. If there are weapons of any kind, then I need to know that before he steps into my house. But that kid looks so strong, he's a weapon all on his own. Why do I get the feeling that this is a monumentally bad idea?*

Mark nodded his head in agreement as he stood back up. But Jordan had other plans. She motioned Cole in the house and said, "Why don't I show you to Mark's room. I can help you unpack."

Cole picked up the duffle bag, and Jordan and Cole started up the stairs. Jordan turned her head toward her brother and stuck out her tongue.

Mark directed his thoughts to Jordan. *If he goes after you, I'm going to let him.*

*Good. I wouldn't have it any other way.*

*Wait! I don't think you know what I meant by "going after you."*

*Either way, I can handle myself.*

# CHAPTER FOUR

## Crisis

*A*fter Cole unpacked, the three of them studied with Jordan's mother. Cole was a senior, and Mark was a junior. Nevertheless, he had to study from Mark's materials for now. Catherine assured him that if things worked out, she would order the books and manuals for his grade level.

Cole was quiet and respectful during the whole lesson. He also seemed to be smart. He was able to answer all of Catherine's questions after hearing the information only once. Jordan looked at him and thought, *How does a boy like this get kicked out of school? He doesn't seem like a troublemaker at all.*

Mark glared at his sister. *This is only his first day. Give him time.*

Cole joined the family for dinner, and again, he was polite and respectful. He thanked Catherine for the food before leaving the table.

"Cole, you will have to tell me what you like to eat if you intend to stay with us," Catherine called out to him.

He turned around and said, "Don't worry. I can fend for myself. I don't want to be a burden to you."

Catherine shook her head. "It's no trouble. It's not like I would cook you a separate meal from everyone else. But I want to know what you like to eat."

Cole looked stunned for a second but then replied, "Whatever everyone else likes." Then he headed up the stairs.

Catherine walked up to Jordan and whispered in her ear, "I really didn't mind having him here today. He seems quite nice."

Jordan smiled, but then Mark screeched his chair back. "I can't believe you two! You honestly can't see beyond his act?" He rose from his chair and stormed off toward his bedroom upstairs.

*What is he going to do?* Jordan decided to follow her brother. He had nothing but dark thoughts about Cole, and she didn't want him to act on any of them.

Mark reached his bedroom door and slammed it open. Cole was sitting on the cot that they had fixed up for him on the opposite side of the bedroom from Mark's bed. Cole didn't bat an eye at the loud noise that the slamming door caused.

"I don't like staying in your room. There is a guest bedroom on this floor. Why don't I stay in there?"

"Because we don't trust you," Mark grunted.

"Okay. But doesn't anyone care about *your* safety?"

"I *really* don't like you."

Cole flashed his eyes at Jordan, who was standing in the doorway. "But your sister does."

*Eep, I could just die right now …*

That did it. Mark lifted Cole off the cot by his collar and slammed him against the bedroom wall. He shoved his forearm into Cole's neck. "If you touch my sister, I'll kill you. Is that understood?"

Jordan ran over to try and break them up but then stopped in her tracks when she noticed Cole's demeanor.

Cole didn't flinch. "Crystal clear." His deep blue eyes looked straight into Mark's, without a hint of emotion.

With a growl, Mark let Cole go. He walked toward his bed and grunted again, "I *really* don't like you."

"You don't have to bother repeating it. I got the idea." Cole returned to his cot.

Catherine appeared at the doorway. "I heard a loud noise. What happened?"

Both boys just looked at each other and shrugged their shoulders.

Catherine then fixed her gaze at Jordan. *What really happened?*

Jordan returned her stare. *They're really not getting along.*

*Then I don't know if this is going to work, Jordan.*

*Mom, it wasn't Cole's fault, it was Mark's.*

Catherine turned her head toward Mark. *What did you do?*

Then Mark smirked. *Why don't you ask Jordan's boyfriend?*

*He's not my boyfriend! Why don't you stop being a jackass?*

Catherine looked over at Cole, who was busy staring at a blank wall. *Yeah, like that would really work ...*

Catherine faced Jordan and said, "Let's leave the two of them alone. They will have to work this out somehow."

"By killing each other?" Jordan asked.

"No. Eventually they will wear each other down. You and Mark did, right? You two don't fight as much as when you were little."

*Oh, Mom. In some ways, we fight even more,* Jordan noted.

*But you two are adult enough that there's no violence. Hopefully we can say the same for those two.*

*I don't know about that ...*

*Well, they're both strong young men. They'll figure it out.*

Jordan nodded and took one last look at Cole. He seemed lost in Mark's room, and she almost felt bad leaving him that way. But this is what he wanted ... or so he said.

When Jordan got to her room and closed the door, she started to get a panic attack. It came on for no reason, but suddenly she could hardly breathe. She clutched her chest and fought the feeling. Her heart felt like it was beating out of her chest. She had an intense throbbing pain inside of her head, and a moment later, she fell to the floor.

She was still conscious but barely. Her vision was blurry.

"Go get your mother! I'll get her to the bed." She could hardly make out Cole's voice.

"No you won't!" Mark warned from a little farther away.

"Just shut up! Maybe your mom will know what to do. Now go!" Jordan felt Cole pick her up and place her gently on the bed.

The next thing Jordan knew, her mother was sitting beside her and placing her hand on Jordan's forehead. "Jordan, can you hear me?"

She could, but that was the last thing she heard.

Within the darkness, she couldn't move. It wasn't like she was paralyzed, but something had her pinned down. She tried to struggle, but the more she did, the firmer the grasp became.

Her eyes flew open, and she screamed. She could hear the sound echo throughout the house.

It seemed like an eternity, but it was probably only a minute until she saw Catherine, Mark, and Cole arrive at her doorway.

She watched as Cole flipped on the lights, and when he did, his eyes grew large as he saw the scene before him. Jordan looked down and saw a shadow-like apparition wrapped around her. The shadow seemed to have long, tentacle-like fingers, and it was using those appendages to grasp Jordan's body from all sides. That way, even the strongest of humans would not be able to break free from its hold.

Nevertheless, Jordan continued to struggle, which only tightened the shadow's grip.

Mark reached out his hands toward her. "Jordan, hold on!" And as his hands were pointed toward her, the shadow stopped moving.

Jordan looked at the shadow, not believing that it stopped. But she was still trapped. She was sweating and shaking, and she just wanted to be free already.

Mark looked at his hands. He was obviously as surprised as everyone else.

Cole walked up to Jordan and placed his hands firmly on each of her shoulders. "Don't worry. I won't let you go. If the shadow takes you, then it will take me too. We're in this together." He then knelt down beside her at the side of the bed.

Jordan stopped shaking for a split second and looked Cole straight in the eyes. For some reason, those deep blue eyes could communicate more than he could ever say. But then she swallowed hard and started shaking again. The shadow was going to move again soon, and now it was going to take them both.

But instead, a sparkling bright light started to encompass Jordan and Cole. It was a tingling sensation, and it was warmer and brighter at the points where the shadow had contact with Jordan's body.

The brighter the light became, the stronger Cole held onto Jordan. The light seemed to be fed by their connection. In shrieks of terror, the shadow burned off into individualized puffs of smoke. Multicolored sparkles descended to the floor as, one by one, the shadows imploded. It seemed that instead of one big shadow, this "thing" was actually comprised of many individual shadows that were interconnected. Cole couldn't see what was going on because he had buried his head against Jordan's shoulder, bracing himself to be taken. But Jordan could, and she was amazed at the colorful display of what was happening in front of her.

Jordan whispered to Cole, "You can get up now."

But Mark was more forceful. He grabbed Cole by the collar and said, "You can get off my sister now."

Cole stood up and looked at everyone. "What happened? I thought we were going to disappear with the shadow."

"Disappear? Why do you think the shadow would make someone disappear?" Catherine asked.

Cole's eyes focused on the floor. "I don't know. Isn't that what shadows do?"

"We wouldn't know. We've never had to deal with a shadow before ... that is ... until you came along." Mark glared at Cole.

"Now, Mark. Cole tried to save Jordan. Why are you still so suspicious of him?" Catherine asked.

"Oh. I don't know. Maybe because all kinds of weird things started happening as soon as he showed up."

"To be fair, weird things started to happen *before* he showed up," Jordan interjected with a very faint voice as she sat up on her bed.

Cole shook his head. "Mark's right. All these bad things started to happen as soon as I arrived. That's been the story of my life. I should just leave."

"No!" Jordan shouted, which was in stark contrast to the whisper she uttered a few seconds before. Then she composed herself and continued in a normal voice, "The shadow didn't disappear until Cole was with me. I want to know what happened between us that caused the shadow to go away."

Cole looked back at Jordan with a serious look on his face. "It must have been a fluke. There's no reason for me to stay."

"I think there is," Catherine said. She cleared her throat and continued, "There was a visible energy emitted when you two connected. I could see it. I think I want to know what that was."

*Oh God, will this nightmare ever end?* Mark thought.

Cole pointed at Mark. "Can you get him to stop doing that? If I have to live in his room, then I would kind of like him to stop having nasty thoughts about me all the time."

*And oh hell, the nightmare just got worse. The hot guy can read our thoughts.* Jordan shook her head.

"Yes, I can. And yours I can deal with. But your brother's are annoying."

# Chapter Five

## Getting Closer

C ole had a vivid dream about Jordan. She was sitting by a lake, wearing a white flower in her hair. Her long blonde waves were blowing in the wind. She looked up and smiled lovingly at him as he approached. She then reached up her lily white hand to him. His unrequited longing for her was so profound that he stood there frozen and was therefore unable to grasp her hand in response.

Something was nudging his shoulder. Cole tried to whack the hand away, but then he cracked one eye open to see who it was. It was Jordan! At the realization, he jumped away from her as quickly as he could.

He was now sleeping in their guest bedroom. Catherine figured that two telepathic teenage boys that didn't like each other probably needed a little space.

"I didn't mean to startle you, but we usually wake up at 8 a.m. It's now 8:30. I thought you would want to get dressed and get something to eat before we start studying."

She sounded and looked sad. Now Cole felt guilty about the reaction that he gave her. She was only trying to be nice. "I'm sorry. I'm always weird when I wake up. I guess I need to buy an alarm clock instead of having you wake me." Jordan shook her head. "That's okay. Get dressed. I'll meet you downstairs." Her smile was back. Cole let out a sigh of relief.

❄ ❄ ❄

Jordan looked up from her bowl of cereal to watch Cole come down the stairs. He had changed into jeans and an orange T-shirt. It seemed that no matter what the outfit, it couldn't conceal his athletic body.

Cole sat down, and Catherine walked up to him. "Cole, what would you like for breakfast?"

"I really don't want you feeding me. I can go to the store and buy my own food."

"Nonsense! Besides, we can talk about that later. If you want your own food, I won't stop you. But until then, what would you like to eat?"

Cole looked around. "What is Mark having?"

Mark stopped mid-bite and pretended he was choking. Catherine giggled and answered, "Pancakes. Do you want some?"

"Sure."

"With syrup?"

"That's fine." Cole stared at his hands. The last thing he wanted to do was put Catherine out. She was so very kind. It was a completely different experience than what he was used to.

Jordan noticed Cole's discomfort. She wanted to help him, but she didn't know how. She realized that it probably was very weird for him to try to fit in with her family. She had never done anything like that before. The poor boy probably felt isolated and alone, even though he was surrounded by other people.

It took a few minutes, but then Catherine set a plate of pancakes in front of Cole. "Anything to drink?"

"Water." Cole gave Catherine a forced smile. She returned with a glass full of ice and water and placed it to the right of his plate.

Then, surprisingly, Catherine sat down. She never did that! Catherine fixed her gaze at Mark. "I have been curious about something since last night." Jordan and Cole sat straight up, but Catherine waved off the two of them. "Not about Jordan and Cole ... yet ... this question is for Mark."

Mark looked at his mother but didn't stop eating. Through his full mouth, he mumbled, "W-what?"

"Honey, it seemed that you froze the shadow last night. How did you cause it to stop moving?"

Mark swallowed and said, "I dunno."

"Well, can you try again?"

Mark seemed to be losing his patience. "What do you want me to freeze?"

Catherine looked around the kitchen. Nothing was moving except the four of them. Then she apparently got an idea. "Freeze Cole."

"Wha—?" But Cole didn't get the whole word out. Mark had lifted his hands and froze him midway. In Jordan's opinion, as he sat there completely motionless, he looked like a statue of a Greek god.

Catherine nodded. "It worked. Now you can let him go."

"That wasn't part of the deal."

"It is now. Let him go!"

Mark huffed. "Fine." He didn't look at Cole but raised his hand, fingers up, and rolled his wrist to release him.

Cole looked around angrily, and Jordan was the first to ask, "How do you know how to do that?"

Mark looked at his sister, appearing like he was deciding if he should tell or not, but then answered, "I practiced this morning, okay? I went outside and tortured all the insects in the backyard."

"You did? Well can you help me practice moving things with my mind? I don't have the slightest idea how to work that."

"I could help you," Cole shyly interjected.

*Oh geez. He's still in the room, and I'm blabbering like an idiot.*

*And ... I can still read your thoughts!* Cole gently laughed as he directed that thought to Jordan.

"Holy crap! How did I end up in a house full of mind-reading people?" Jordan asked.

"Watch your language," Catherine admonished her daughter. But the smile on her face as she turned toward the sink gave away her true feelings about Jordan's situation.

"Well, it's a good thing that Cole can read our minds. That way I don't even have to open my mouth to insult him. How ... convenient," Mark said.

"Yeah. But I can turn my telepathy off. So either way, I can still ignore you."

"You can turn it off? How?" Mark asked.

Catherine turned back from the sink and asked, "Cole, what else can you do?"

Cole looked like he choked on his pancake. Catherine waved her hand at him. "Never mind. Let's go outside. I have something specific that I want you to show me."

Cole was lagging behind the others in finishing his breakfast, so he shoveled the rest of his food in his mouth and grabbed his things. Then the four of them went out the side door and headed to the backyard.

They all congregated in the middle of the yard, and Catherine had Cole and Jordan stand side by side. "Cole, I want to see what happened with you and Jordan last night."

"Me? How should I know? I didn't even see what happened!"

Jordan looked over at Cole with a smile on her face. "I did, and it was pretty awesome!"

Cole couldn't help but smile as he looked at his feet, but he answered, "Well, that may be, but I still don't know *how* it happened."

"I have a theory," Catherine interjected. "Have you ever heard of the concept of yin/yang?"

Cole shook his head, and Jordan just looked at her mother with a confused expression.

Catherine bent down and picked up a notebook that she had brought outside. She drew something in it for a minute and then stood up and showed Jordan, Cole, and Mark the symbol she had drawn.

Catherine then stood in front of the three teenagers and pointed to the symbol. "Yin/yang—male/female, light/dark—opposites attract. This theory balances two different energies together into one symbiotic whole. I say 'symbiotic' because the two energies benefit from each other and become stronger than the sum of the two separate parts. Yin/yang is always equal and opposite working together."

"Aw, Mom. Jordan thinks that she is supposed to be pretty bad-ass. Why would Cole be her equal?" Mark asked.

Catherine smiled. "I'm thinking that Cole is pretty *bad-ass* on his own."

Jordan remembered her dream. *I don't think we've even scratched the surface of Cole's powers.*

Cole looked over at Jordan with a concerned look on his face. But before he could ask what she meant by that, Catherine said, "Jordan, Cole ... hold hands."

"What? You want Jordan to hold his hand?" Mark huffed.

"Yes I do. He was holding her shoulders last night."

Mark didn't say another word. He just stood there with his arms crossed against his chest.

Cole looked down at his hands but did not make the first move. Jordan gave him a reassuring smile and slowly reached out her hand to his. He looked at her with hesitation in his eyes but then took her hand into his own.

"Okay, I want you two to concentrate. Last night was an emergency situation. So we can't simulate that completely. Not that I'd even want to. But visualize connecting on a spiritual level."

*How the heck do I do that?* Jordan looked over at Cole. He gave her hand a little squeeze to let her know he was ready.

Jordan closed her eyes and concentrated on her breathing. A couple of seconds later, she could feel it. The warmth and intensity flowing from Cole was taking her over. It felt like an electrical current, but it didn't cause her to panic. Instead, his energy surged through her body at a pace that matched her own energy's natural rhythm. There was no doubt that the power emanating from Cole was exceptionally strong. But hers matched his completely, almost as if they were specifically created for each other.

Cole and Jordan had their eyes closed, but Catherine and Mark could see what was happening. When the two of them connected, a massive funnel of pure energy radiated from where they were standing. Clouds began to form, and Catherine looked up at the sky with concern. A huge thunder clap sounded over the backyard, and a burst of energy exploded between Cole and Jordan. The blast threw them back several feet in opposite directions.

After witnessing this, Catherine remembered Jordan's ability to control the weather. She had studied the concept of yin/yang and knew about its potential to magnify the power that people have. Nevertheless, she didn't count on it being able to cause this type of reaction from the elements around them. She decided that adding anyone's powers to Jordan's, with her atmokinesis ability, may not be such a great idea after all.

"Okay ... that's enough. Let's go inside. Cole can tell us about telepathy in there." Catherine headed toward the house, and Mark followed her.

Cole walked over toward Jordan to help her up. "That was really something, huh?"

He flashed an enthusiastic, baby-faced grin and held out his hand to her as she continued to sit on the ground. She reached out to take his hand, and at the moment they touched, she saw a huge flash of light in her mind. The next thing she saw was a woman sitting in front of a mirror, gazing at herself. Then she looked down at her neck. The necklace that Theia gave her was hanging there, just like it was before.

She looked back toward the mirror, and her amber colored eyes stared back at her. She had long, thick black hair, which was pulled back by a gold crown. She wore a long, white dress with a jeweled neckline, and her arms were tanned in a caramel-type color. Before she could review herself any further, her assistant appeared in a nearby doorway and beckoned for her to follow.

*Where am I?* Jordan thought to herself. But she stood up and followed the young woman down a pathway that led to the pharaoh. *Pharaoh? Did I suddenly travel back in time somehow?* Jordan approached him, and as she drew closer, she also recognized him. He had a dark tan and long, straight, black hair. Otherwise, she could plainly see in his eyes that it was Mark. His face did not contain any trace of humor in it, and Jordan realized that the weight of the throne must have torn out any amount of levity that his personality would have otherwise contained. Jordan then proceeded to sit next to him. She realized that she was Mark's daughter in this lifetime.

Jordan looked over and saw an attractive young woman approach the pharaoh. The woman knelt to the side and whispered in the pharaoh's ear. Afterward, the young woman looked over in Jordan's direction. Those eyes, unmistakably Catherine's, were so full of love. Jordan realized that Catherine was the pharaoh's spiritual advisor. This post was usually held by a man but was given to her instead due to her extraordinary visions. She was the pharaoh's cousin and had been by his side since they were children.

At that point, Jordan looked over to her other side, where a very handsome, young man sat. He was tan and muscular with jet black, long, thick hair and huge black eyes. She stared at him as he stoically gazed out in front of him. He then caught her glance out of the corner of his eye. He first looked at her curiously but then reached out for her hand, and a grin grew up from his lips and encompassed his whole face. The expression turned into the same baby-faced grin that Cole was giving her before she got caught up in this vision. Suddenly, she realized that Cole had been her husband in ancient Egypt, and his smile was what brought her back to the memory of that lifetime. That realization abruptly snapped her back to the present.

And ... Cole was still holding her hand ...

Jordan was shaking, but Cole had a firm grip on her. Her hand glowed pearl white, and then she noticed that the aura encompassed her entire body.

She turned to face Cole. He looked worried but not shocked.

"What happened?" he asked softly.

*He can read minds!*

"You didn't see it?"

Cole looked confused. "See what? Didn't you black out?"

*He didn't see it! Or he's lying. Either way, I'm out of here.*

"Nothing—it was nothing!" She pulled her hand away, and before he could stop her, she ran toward the house without him.

# CHAPTER SIX

# Reaching Out from Beyond Time

*J* ordan ran in the side door of her house and quickly looked around. As soon as she saw Catherine, Jordan rushed over to her and said, "Dad's family stuff is in the attic, right?"

"Yeah, I think so," Catherine answered with a confused look on her face.

"Let's go." Jordan grabbed her mother's hand and dragged her up the stairs.

Once they arrived in the attic, Catherine asked, "What's this all about?"

Jordan took hold of her amulet. "I'm going to find out about this. Dad has to have something about Great-Grandmother in all this stuff."

"But, honey, everything is written in Ukrainian. What good is it if you can't read it?"

Jordan shook her head. "I have to find something."

The two of them came across a couple of boxes, and Jordan quickly sifted through them. The second box was full of books, and Jordan looked through each one briefly until she found one that had a hard, dark emerald green cover with the symbol matching Jordan's amulet etched on the front. The symbol was embossed in gold and still brilliant, even through the dust and wearing.

Jordan opened the book, and there it was—just what she was looking for. On the first page was a picture of a young woman that bore a striking resemblance to herself. And the young woman was wearing Jordan's amulet.

*That has to be my great-grandmother. There's no doubt about it. But how do we look so much alike?*

Catherine scooted over so that she could sit right next to Jordan. That way, both of them could look at the book at the same time. Jordan flipped the page, and after the photograph on the first page, the rest of the book was all written in Ukrainian. There was absolutely no hope of her being able to read it right now.

Catherine noticed Jordan's downtrodden look and reached over to place her hand on her daughter's shoulder. "What do you want to do now? I can tell this was important to you."

Jordan felt like she was going to cry, but she couldn't. Something was holding her back from expressing her feelings. Maybe it was that she was afraid. If she allowed herself to feel the full weight of the last few days, she would break down. And she couldn't have that.

"Mom, everything is revolving around this necklace. I need to know why Great-Grandmother gave it to me. My life has turned upside down, and I need to know why!"

Jordan looked back at the large, emerald green covered book that was sitting on her lap. She flipped back to the page with the picture of her great-grandmother. "This book has the answers. I know it does ..."

"*You* have the answers," a hushed woman's voice sounded behind Jordan. The voice echoed as if it were traveling through the wind, even though they were inside the house.

Jordan looked behind her, but no one was there. Then she turned to face her mother. "Did you hear that?"

Catherine nodded but was too stunned to actually say anything.

Jordan closed the book, placed it gently on the ground, and then stood up. She scanned the room for whatever it was that just uttered those words.

From out of nowhere, a white mist swirled in front of Jordan. Her vision blurred from the mist, so Jordan blinked her eyes a couple of times. Once she could focus again, she saw a young woman step toward her.

It was the young woman from the picture, and looking at her was like looking into a mirror for Jordan. The only difference was that the person before her seemed to be in her mid-twenties, and Jordan was only thirteen. But other than that, the two were very similar. She was wearing Jordan's amulet and had on a long, white dress that reached down to her ankles. Beyond the dress, she was barefoot. She also had the mysterious pearl-white glow that Jordan remembered in her dream.

*Okay, why should this surprise me? Everything else in my life is driving me crazy. So why not have dead relatives that look just like me stare me in the face? This shouldn't even faze me right now.*

The figure standing in front of Jordan was rigid with a serious expression on her face. "I see that you've been reunited with the amulet and our book. That's good."

Jordan looked at the book with the amulet's symbol on it. "*Our* book? What do you mean by that?"

"I wrote it for you. That way you would have my instructions when you needed it."

"Great ... just great ... you wrote it in Ukrainian. How am I supposed to read it?"

Catherine stood up. "And how are you talking to us in English?"

The young woman answered, "I've crossed over. Spirit communicates in whatever language that will be understood."

"And again ... that's just great. But how does that help me read *our* book?"

The young woman diverted her eyes from Catherine to Jordan. "The book is made of pure energy. It can be manipulated in order for you to understand."

"What, what—*what*? What do you mean by that?" Jordan asked with a perturbed look on her face.

"Ask Theia. She will help you."

"I'm sick and tired of you and Theia talking to me in riddles! You two are the only ones who know what's going on, so why not tell it to me straight? I don't want to guess anymore. I just want the truth already!" Jordan blurted out.

"And what is *the* truth when the universe is infinite?"

*Ugh ... my head just exploded.* "Okay. Well, why are you here? I don't need you to spit out questions to *me*! So why don't you go back to wherever you came from and leave me alone? I'll just find someone, like Dad, to translate your book."

Catherine's eyes lit up at Jordan's last statement. "How much of all this does Victor know?"

"All of it," the woman said.

Jordan's mom looked like she was going to be sick. But that didn't stop Jordan's tirade. "Well, that's good. I'll just ask him."

The woman looked at Jordan with a sad expression. "Jordan, I can't go just yet. I need you to do something for me. Catherine, can you get the two boys?"

Catherine looked at the great-grandmother and clarified, "Mark and Cole?"

The great-grandmother nodded.

"Why?" Catherine asked.

"I need them. Can you please just do it for me?"

Catherine let out a deep sigh. She looked around for a second and then asked, "Why Cole? He isn't a part of this."

"You'll sec. Please go. I need to talk to Jordan while you get them."

Catherine looked at the two identical women, one older and one younger, and then nodded. She hurried out of the attic and down the stairs.

The great-grandmother fixed her stare at Jordan. "I know this is hard for you. That's why I asked that you not get the amulet until you turn thirteen."

"Hmpf. Any age would be too young for all this."

"I understand how you feel. But I held it off as long as I could. Believe me."

"Why should I? You haven't given me any reason *to* believe you!"

The young woman opened her mouth to answer Jordan but was interrupted by Catherine, Mark, and Cole entering the attic. The woman turned and looked specifically at the two boys.

"Hello, Mark."

Mark almost fell over himself. *Who age-progressed Jordan?*

Cole, for his part, kept on looking back and forth between Jordan and her older version. He had a confused look on his face, but he didn't say a word.

For the first time since she appeared, a small smile set in on the young woman's face. "And hello Cole. It's been awhile. I've really missed you."

# CHAPTER SEVEN

# Revelation

"J-Jordan ... what's going on?" Cole asked.

Jordan hesitated for a second, but then with new resolve, she turned toward Cole and said, "You tell me. She seems to know you."

"I thought she was you! I thought that you cloned yourself."

"What? How in the heck would I do that? Don't be ridiculous."

"It's not ridiculous. And in a way, that's exactly what happened," the spirit interjected in a serious tone.

Jordan faced her. "What are you saying?"

"What do you think I'm saying?"

"I think ... that you talk in riddles!"

The young woman pinched the bridge of her nose for a second and then said, "Oh, Jordan. Why do we have to begin again every time we come in? Why can't all the information that we obtain in a lifetime follow us to the next?"

"Um ... okay ... the next time *you* ask *me* a question, I'm gonna use my telekinesis to throw you out the window."

"No you won't."

"How do you know?" Jordan asked.

"Easy."

"I'm thinking of ways to torture you in my mind."

The spirit smiled. "I know."

"How? You're telepathic too?"

"Yes, but there is another way I know."

"And that is?"

"You're me, and I'm you," the spirit answered.

*And brain function just came to a halt.* Jordan glanced over at her mother, who looked a little shocked at first, but then her normal expression took over.

"What do you mean by that?"

The woman sighed. "Jordan, you already know about reincarnation. Why do you even ask?"

"Because ... you're *nothing* like me!"

The great-grandmother let out a frustrated laugh. "Oh, really?"

"No way. All I need is two of them! One is bad enough," Mark declared. He had been standing at the doorway next to Cole during this whole back-and-forth conversation. But now he decided to go in and find a box to sit on.

"Mark, shut up!" Jordan screamed while not even looking at him.

Jordan directed her attack back at her great-grandmother. "Okay, fine. You're me from a different lifetime. But, if that's the case, then how can I have a conversation with you?"

"Bilocation. Souls can be in multiple places at once. Right, Cole?"

Cole started to back away toward the doorway, but Jordan wouldn't let him. "Hold it! Where do you think you're going? I still want to know how you know my great-grandmother."

"That's your great-grandmother? Well, she's dead right? That explains the white aura, huh?"

"Stalling?" Jordan asked.

The young woman stepped forward to try to reassure Jordan. "Don't pester him. He really doesn't know what I'm talking about." She placed her hand on Jordan's shoulder and continued, "He didn't meet *me* until he met *you* yesterday."

"Then why did you say it's been awhile?"

The great-grandmother laughed under her breath. "Hmm ... I think the last lifetime we shared was back in Rome—right, Cole?"

Cole looked stunned. He was almost as motionless as when Mark froze him in the morning.

"Or should I say, Romulus?"

Catherine, who had since sat down at the side of the room, gaped at what the great-grandmother said. "Romulus?" Catherine took a deep breath. "Romulus, as in the man who founded Rome?"

"Yes."

"Romulus, who was the son of Mars, the Roman god of war?"

"That's the one."

"Wasn't Romulus deified upon his death and became the Roman god Quirinus?"

At that point, Jordan stole another look at Cole. He still wasn't moving. *I thought that he looked like a statue of a Greek god. Silly me—I was so far off!*

"Yes," the great-grandmother answered.

"How can a god be standing in front of us like this?"

The young woman replied, "How are any of us standing here like this? All of us are connected in spirit. We are all one. None of us are higher or lower in the chain of command. All of us are doing our part to make the universe a better place—for ourselves, each other, and our creator.

"But as for Cole ... he made a conscious decision to be here. For eons, it was more important for him to be in the spiritual realm. But now it's different. The Crystal Children have been sent. And because of this, there have been great shifts in spiritual beings cycling through the planet. Gods, goddesses, incarnated angels, Atlanteans ... they are all here now. And they all have an important purpose in being here. Change is now, and all the heavy hitters are in the physical realm to promote this change."

The woman smiled again. "Besides, it was no accident that Cole and Jordan were reunited. That was a part of our plan from the very beginning."

"I need to sit down," Jordan said as she walked over to the side of the room, next to her mother.

But along the way, Jordan couldn't help but notice Cole. He was still standing there, completely stunned. He couldn't move at that moment, even if he wanted to.

*Great ... she broke the hot guy! I don't think I'll ever forgive her. Oh ... wait ... I guess that means I'll never forgive myself? Yikes! Now I'm confused!*

"Um, by the way, if you and I are the same person, then how do you know so much? I certainly don't know any of this!"

"You've forgotten. Give it time. It will all come back to you."

Catherine asked the young woman, "Do people really remember all of their past lives?"

"No, just me."

"Ugh! What else can I do?" Jordan asked. She was now seated on a box next to her mother. Mark was seated on the opposite side of the room, and the great-grandmother was standing in the middle of everyone. Cole hadn't moved from his place in front of the doorway.

"I'm sure you'll find out."

"Riddles again? Why?"

"Haven't I told you enough?"

"No. Why don't you tell me why you're here now? You told mom to fetch Mark and Cole. Why was that necessary?"

"Because I need the four of you to come back with me to my lifetime."

And that did it ...

"Wait a minute! You said that we needed to be here—to protect the Crystal Children! Why would we go back in time with you?"

"Because it will improve things on your side as well."

Jordan glared at her older counterpart. Neither of them spoke for a second, so Jordan responded, "I'm ... listening!"

The great-grandmother hesitated at first but then continued, "It's a personal favor to me. Okay? Is that a good enough reason?"

Cole had started moving and was actively eyeing the doorway again. Jordan called out to him, "Why don't you come over here and sit down? You've been looking awkward this whole time!"

Mark grumbled, "Wow. He *chose* to be with *you*? For a Roman god, he's not that bright."

Cole didn't have any fight within him, so he just slowly walked over and sat down beside Jordan. But Jordan wasn't going to let Mark's comment go. She looked straight at her great-grandmother and said, "Please tell me that one of my powers is the ability to shut him up. Because *that* would really be useful!"

The young woman raised her hand. "Yours are much better." Then she shifted her stance slightly. "But please. Let's get back to the favor."

She looked directly at Jordan. "I lived in Ukraine during the early part of the twentieth century. A few years before World War II, a famine plagued our country. It killed many, many people. And one of them ... was a Crystal Scout."

Catherine asked, "What's a Crystal Scout?"

"It's a sole Crystal Child that was sent to see if the world was ready for the shift. Since the child was killed, the rest of the children didn't start coming until your lifetime."

Catherine said, "So you want us to save the child so that the shift could start sooner? Wouldn't that change history?"

"It would, but only in a positive manner. The bulk of the Crystal Children will still be born to your generation. But if this Crystal Scout is able to live, then the generations in between can better prepare for the shift that is happening to your lives right now."

"This isn't against some sort of *cosmic rule*?"

"Don't worry, Catherine. I have already cleared this with the powers that be," the spirit answered.

"Yippee! I can hardly wait to go back to the past and get ourselves killed. *How* do we do that exactly?" Mark asked.

"We use Cole's bilocation ability to get there."

# CHAPTER EIGHT

## Journey to the Past

C ole cleared his throat and said, "I think you have me mistaken with someone else."

The spirit stood firm. "I don't think so."

"I'm not who you think I am."

"Oh, really?"

Cole stood up. "I'm in the wrong place. I should really leave."

The young woman with the glowing white aura approached him and placed her hand on his cheek. "Cole, how is your wolf doing?"

Cole stepped away from her. "M-my wolf?"

"You know what I'm talking about."

Cole placed his hand on the cheek she just touched. "How do you know about my spirit guide? Even my guardian doesn't know."

"Because I know *you*." The young woman tried to give him a reassuring smile. "Do you know how you found her?"

"*She* found *me* ... after I was adopted."

"In this lifetime, yes."

And then a realization showed through Catherine's eyes. "Oh my God. Don't tell me that's the wolf that saved Romulus and Remus from death when they were babies."

"That's right. Just like a mother, she's never left him. Even after all this time."

"What are you two talking about?" Cole asked as he looked back and forth between them.

Catherine faced him. "There was a legend that Romulus's uncle tried to drown him and his twin brother. But a she-wolf saved them and raised the two boys as her own for a few years before they were discovered by a shepherd."

Mark suddenly stood up. "Wait a minute. I think I remember this story! Didn't Romulus *kill* Remus?"

The young woman answered, "He did. But he had his reasons."

Cole sat back down. "*Now,* I want to drown myself."

"That would be stupid. Then all the centuries you spent improving would go to waste," the young woman countered.

"Okay then, I'm gonna be sick."

"You don't have time. We need you."

Cole squinted his eyes at her. "What's your name? You know, since you know so much about me."

"Jordan Ivanov, of course."

"My ... name?" Jordan squeaked.

The older Jordan turned to glance directly at her younger counterpart. "What did you think? I asked Victor to name you after me."

"Is there anything else I need to know?" Jordan asked.

"Not for now."

"So let's get this over with!" Jordan declared.

The young woman shifted her eyes to look at Cole. "I need you to sit down on the floor, in the middle of the room."

"I don't know what you have in mind. My bilocation doesn't work that way."

"It will. This time, you have me and Jordan helping you. Please sit." She motioned for him to sit on the floor by her feet. Then she sat down beside him to the right and took his hand. She fixed her gaze at Jordan. "Sit on his other side and hold his hand."

Jordan stood up. "If he's here for me, I don't know how I like you holding his hand."

"You're jealous of yourself?" the spirit asked.

"Yeah, and I know it's kind of weird. Because losing a guy to yourself would be a real drag."

"Can we go before *I* get sick?" Mark blurted out.

The older version of Jordan smiled and motioned her head toward her younger counterpart. "Mark, go sit next to Jordan and take her hand. Catherine," she looked over at Jordan's mom, "sit next to me. We will all be connected through the transfer."

Mark and Catherine sat down, and everyone held hands in a circle. Jordan looked over, and Cole had a very scared look on his face. He turned his head to the older Jordan and said, "I-I don't know what to do."

She gave him an encouraging smile. "You don't have to. Just close your eyes and relax. I will walk you through it."

To Jordan, Cole didn't look like he would be able to relax. He looked as stiff as a board. Then the great-grandmother continued, "I want you to visualize a small, one-story wooden house at the end of a long, winding dirt road. There is a living room inside, with a circular area rug in front of a fireplace. Cole, I want you to take us there."

Cole shut his eyes tighter, and then he opened them. His eyes were glowing bright orange, and the rest of his body was suddenly surrounded by a pearl-white aura. Jordan turned to look at her great-grandmother. She was surrounded by the same aura, but her eyes were glowing cerulean blue.

Jordan looked down at her hand that was holding Cole's, and she had started glowing as well. It seemed that the aura was emanating out from her great-grandmother toward everyone else in the circle. Jordan felt the energy that seemed to come from everyone else surge through her body. The vibration of it was pulling her under some sort of fog. She couldn't have fought free even if she had tried. Before she knew it, the feeling was gone. She opened her eyes, and they were there. It was just as her great-grandmother had described.

Jordan stood up to take in her surroundings. They were definitely not at home. This place reeked of death, to the point that it was unbearable. The air was stale and heavy. It was hard to breathe.

Jordan walked up to her brother and pinched him.

"Ow! What was that for?" Mark asked.

"I just wanted to make sure I wasn't dreaming."

"Don't you pinch *yourself* when that happens?"

"I wanted you to be sure too."

Mark huffed and stood up next to his sister but turned to face her older version. "How does Cole do that? What is bilocation anyway?"

The great-grandmother stood up and brushed herself off. "As I said, souls can be in two places at once—or for that matter, multiple places at once. But, what Cole has never done before is use it to move within time. That ... he needed my help for."

"Do you move in and out of time a lot?" Jordan asked.

"When I need to." The great-grandmother was now wearing a dress that was more appropriate to her time. It was somewhat torn and dirty, but it covered her up to her neck and down to her ankles. The sleeves extended to her wrists but had tiny holes bored into them along the way.

Catherine got up and walked over to the one small window and pulled aside the curtain. As she looked out at the village, Jordan could see the sadness on her face. Jordan slowly stepped over to the window, so that she could see what her mother was looking at.

It was devastating. The other houses looked even more in disrepair than the one they were standing in. There was one villager that was walking down the dirt road that seemed to connect all the houses and village together. He looked painfully thin, like a walking corpse. The energy that it took for him to walk a short distance was causing him to be out of breath, to the point of passing out. Jordan turned her head to look at her mother, just in time to see a tear well up in the corner of her eye.

"I could never say anything that could prepare you for this," the great-grandmother called out. "The people that are left in the village are doing everything they can to survive."

Cole stood up and started looking around the house. "Where is the child we're supposed to save?"

The great-grandmother glanced over at Cole. "He's in the wheat field trying to get some food. He was killed for stealing."

"What? There are wheat fields here, when people are dying of hunger?" Catherine asked from over at her spot next to the window.

"Yes. The food is being sent elsewhere."

"How can that be? Why doesn't anyone stop that from happening?" Catherine looked like she was going to start crying.

"There are soldiers everywhere. And they aren't dying of hunger. How do you suppose we fight them?" the great-grandmother asked.

Catherine looked down at the floor. "I guess … you can't."

"But we can!" Cole interjected.

Jordan thought, *Hey! He finally found his voice!*

The great-grandmother shook her head. "Impossible. You are here to save one life. You don't live here. You can't save them all. Besides, most of them are already dead."

Cole's head dropped down again, and the helpless expression was overwhelming his normally handsome features.

*What good is it that we're supposed to be all-powerful, yet we are completely helpless in these surroundings? It doesn't make any sense!*

The great-grandmother looked over at Jordan and answered her unspoken question, "We were sent to spread peace, one soul at a time. What we are doing now is saving that one soul. Believe me; it will cause a ripple effect that will benefit us all."

"Sure thing. So where is this wheat field?" Cole asked.

The great-grandmother motioned him to the one table, toward the kitchen. She quickly drew a basic map of the village and put an X at the spot that she expected the boy to be in.

Mark walked over and asked, "How will we recognize him?"

With a serious stare, the great-grandmother answered, "He's the one that's about to be killed."

# Chapter Nine

## Rescue

C ole walked to the door and grabbed the handle, but before he turned it, he looked back to the rest of the group. Jordan, Catherine, and Mark were following him, but the great-grandmother was still standing in the same spot. She was looking down at her hands as she nervously rubbed them together.

"Are you coming?" Cole asked.

"Yes, but I will be lagging behind a bit. I was advised that I could be killed if I intervened personally."

"And we can't?" Jordan questioned with a perturbed expression.

"You guys will be stronger when it comes to fighting. I wasn't sent to Earth to fight."

"Maybe we should put Cole upfront like a shield. After all, he is a god," Mark observed.

The great-grandmother shook her head. "Oh, no. He was a god. He's human now. He could very well die."

"Great," Cole muttered. He turned the doorknob and proceeded out the door.

Jordan looked back at her great-grandmother for a moment but then followed Cole. Catherine and Mark went out the door together.

As Jordan walked down that same dirt road she had seen through the window, she closed her eyes for a second. She could hear the others' thoughts, and her mind was racing with the potential impact that this action could have on her family ... and ... Cole.

Why was Cole doing this? Her great-grandmother was convinced he was involved. But was he? This wasn't his family they were talking about. Why would he care?

She looked up at the blond young man who was leading their group, and she respected his unspoken decision to help. She knew he wasn't happy about it, but he agreed anyway. He obviously had a good heart.

And the rest of her family? Had they gone completely insane? They could all be killed! She looked back to see if the great-grandmother was following them, and if she was, Jordan couldn't see her. *Isn't that something? She asks for our help, and she doesn't even come along! She can't be me. I would never do anything like that!*

Cole kept looking at the map as he walked. It took about fifteen minutes to reach their destination. Finally, he turned to the rest of the group and pointed. "There's the wheat field."

Mark looked around. "This looks familiar." He cocked his head toward the right corner of the field. "Did you hear that?"

The rest of them shook their heads, but he didn't stand around waiting for their answer. Mark took off in the direction of the sound he had just heard.

Jordan ran after her brother, dodging the stalks of wheat in her way, with Catherine and Cole following close behind. As she got closer, she could make out the silhouette of a figure right in front of Mark. But a couple of seconds later, that silhouette stopped moving.

She caught up to her brother and surveyed the area. A young boy, about five years old, was lying unconscious on the ground. A Russian soldier was standing over the boy with his gun pointed at him. The bullet was suspended in midair between the gun and the little boy's chest.

"He hit the boy over the head with the back of his rifle," Mark commented in a sad tone. He looked like he was going to cry. Jordan wondered when he suddenly got so emotional.

Jordan waved her hand and sent the bullet flying away from the young boy. At the same time, Catherine sat down next to the boy and stroked his straight brown hair out of his face to expose the wound that the soldier's rifle had inflicted.

Suddenly, the soldier unfroze to see the four of them with the little boy.

*How did he unfreeze? Mark hadn't released him, so how did he get free?*

A confused expression crossed the soldier's face, but he quickly regained his composure. He took a step back to ready his rifle. He then pointed the gun directly at Jordan.

Cole jumped over and pushed Jordan out of the way. The bullet missed. But then the soldier turned his gun back to the little boy. He shot again, and this time Catherine shielded the little boy with her body. The bullet pierced her back, and her whole body went limp. She keeled over toward the boy, with her body still shielding him.

"Mom!" Jordan shouted. Cole had her pinned down and wasn't letting go. He was physically blocking her from the range of the soldier's bullets. But in her mind, that was the last thing she wanted or needed at the moment.

She looked around and saw Mark standing there. He was obviously taking in the scene around him. Mom was down and covering the child. Cole was protecting Jordan. And ... there was still a soldier with a loaded rifle!

Mark lifted his hands and froze the soldier again. But this time, he wrenched the rifle out of his grasp and tossed the weapon several feet away. Mark clocked him square in the nose, thus shattering it completely. Then, Mark waived his hand in the air to unfreeze the soldier.

The soldier lifted his hands to cover his bloody nose, but he didn't react to the pain as Jordan would have expected. He looked straight at Mark, and suddenly, the soldier's eyes turned dark red. Even though the soldier couldn't have been more than eighteen years old, his face no longer held any remnants of innocence.

"Mark's in trouble," Cole observed, and in an instant, a copy of Cole appeared behind the soldier. Cole grabbed the young man's neck from behind with one arm and pulled the soldier's right arm behind his back using the other. He was trying to keep the man from moving, but then a smile crossed the soldier's face.

Cole couldn't see it, but Jordan could. It was a creepy smile. *Bloody nose, blood red eyes, and an unnerving smile equals ... danger!*

"Cole!" Jordan screamed. But it was too late. Cole jumped back and looked down at his arms. He had second-degree burns where his skin had contact with the soldier.

The soldier then looked over to one side, where Mark was standing, and to the other where Cole was. He then disappeared in a whirlwind of smoke.

The two boys looked around for a second, but then the copy of Cole disappeared. The Cole that was still with Jordan looked at her and then lifted his arms again to survey the burn marks.

"Wait a minute. The Cole over there got burned. How are you burned over here?" Jordan asked.

"What do you mean? They're all me. I can't escape anything that happens to one of my copies. The only thing that doesn't happen is me getting killed. You would have to kill off each and every one of *me* to do that."

"Okay ..."

Mark went over to his mother. She was still breathing but unconscious. He carefully lifted her up off the boy, mindful of the gunshot wound, and cradled her in his arms. "Hold her so that she's sitting up," a voice came from behind Mark. He craned his head around, and his whole body stiffened up. But when he saw where the voice came from, he visibly relaxed. It was the great-grandmother.

"Thank you for your help," Mark muttered.

"You're welcome. Now do what I asked."

Mark grunted but held the top half of his mother's body so that she would be in a sitting position.

"I'm glad that she's unconscious, because otherwise this would hurt like hell." The great- grandmother sat down beside Catherine and put her hand directly on the gunshot wound. There was a thump, and a whole bunch of blood spurted out from the wound, but then the great-grandmother looked at the bullet that was now in her hand.

She dropped the bloody thing and then put her hand a couple of inches from the blood-drenched hole in Catherine's back. She closed her eyes and started to glow pearl white. She was slowly breathing in and out, and then she opened her eyes again. She flashed her cerulean blue orbs toward the wound. A vortex of white light emanated from her hand and attached itself to Catherine's injury. Within seconds, the wound sealed up. Her back looked like nothing had ever happened. The only thing that betrayed the fact that she was ever shot was that her clothes were still stained red, and the hole in her shirt remained.

Catherine's eyes fluttered open, and she looked up into Mark's hazel eyes. Then she looked around and saw the unconscious child at her side. "Did we save him?"

"He's still unconscious, but he'll live," the great-grandmother responded.

"When did you get here?"

"Just in time."

"Pffttt!" Mark sputtered out.

"Cole, I'll get your burned arms later. For now, we have to get going." The great-grandmother looked around and then hesitantly stood up. "Follow me." She bent down to pick up the unconscious boy and waved her hand to beckon the rest of the group to go in the opposite direction from which they came.

They made their way through the wheat field and out the other side to a forested area. Out of the corner of her eye, Jordan spotted the dirt road, and she unconsciously hurried toward it.

Her great-grandmother tried to stop her, but it was too late. As Jordan's foot touched the dirt road, a truck abruptly stopped a few yards from her. Three soldiers filed out of the vehicle, rifles in hand.

The soldiers readied their rifles, and the rest of the group caught up with Jordan. The great-grandmother kept back toward the forest, but Cole and Mark stood on either side of where Jordan was positioned. Catherine placed herself in front of Jordan.

When the bullets started coming their way, Catherine raised her hands to block her face. Suddenly, the bullets stopped and went flying back to the soldiers quicker than when they were discharged from the guns. The soldiers had to duck and move out of the way to avoid getting hit.

Catherine looked at her hands in amazement but then quickly composed herself and got back in the same position. If that motion worked, then she certainly wasn't going to move and let her children get killed.

Cole turned to Jordan. "I don't want to freak you out, but I'm ending this." Jordan didn't know what that meant, but it didn't take too long to find out.

Cole started glowing pearl white, and his eyes flashed orange again. Then he held out his hand toward the soldiers, and a blast of fire shot out from his wrist. He directed the flames to create a wall of fire between their group and the enemy, in the hope that would deter them.

The three men stared at the flames but did not seem bothered. Their eyes changed to a blood-red color like the eyes of the first soldier. Then they proceeded to walk straight through the fire.

*I need to do something! What should I do?* Jordan took a long look at Cole. *He seems super-charged when he starts glowing. How do I do that?* She reached out and touched his shoulder. She could feel the vibration of the energy coursing through his body. *How do I tap into my own energy? There must be a way!*

She closed her eyes and started hyperventilating. But then she remembered that she needed to relax. She slowed her breathing and tried to concentrate on it. She looked down at her hands, and there it was. The pearl-white glow was starting to wrap around her as well.

But something else was happening in her hands. In her palms, there was a static type of energy. It was the cerulean blue color but looked like electrical sparks. Cole turned to see what she was doing. "Here, let me help you with that."

Cole called over to Mark, "Freeze them. I have an idea."

Mark nodded and lifted his hands. The three soldiers immediately stopped moving, within the flames. "They won't stay frozen for long."

"I know." Cole then placed his hands gently over Jordan's. He put her two hands together, palm to palm, and then breathed, "Concentrate. Concentrate on the sparks. Envision them shaping into a sphere within your hands."

"What?" Jordan whispered. But she looked down at her hands and tried to do what he said. Within seconds, she started to pull her hands apart, and a cerulean blue orb appeared.

Cole smiled and lifted his hand. Within a few seconds, a matching orange orb appeared. "Now go!" Cole threw his energy sphere toward the truck. The vehicle exploded, and the blast flung the three soldiers in the air. But when they hit the ground, they unfroze. All three started to get up, and it was apparent that the men were still headed toward the line of people in front of them.

Jordan was stunned. She was holding her orb, but she couldn't move.

"I told you to go!" Cole screamed.

She threw the orb, but because she was so nervous, the orb missed the soldier she was aiming for. It blew open the ground next to the man, but the impact wasn't enough to knock him off his feet. Jordan just shook her head. She was never good at sports, and this just seemed like high-stakes baseball. The game they were playing right now ... she was sure to lose.

Then Mark turned to Jordan. He grabbed her by the shoulders and started to shake her. "Snap out of it. You told me you're strong, and I believe you now. Try your weather technique!"

Jordan could feel her eyes bugging out of her head. Mark finally believed in her, and she didn't want to let him down. Besides, the consequences were too high for her to fail. She started looking at the sky. What type of weather could she summon that would possibly stop creepy demon-looking men that could evidently walk through fire?

And then she got it.

With a determined look, Jordan raised her right arm and started rotating it in front of her. From behind the soldiers, a tornado funnel started to form. As Jordan's outstretched hand rotated faster and faster, the funnel gained speed and headed directly for the soldiers. Before they could move, they were swept into the deadly wind. Then Jordan flung her right hand in front of her, and the funnel swept away, far enough that it was out of their range of vision.

"I don't want to be around if they somehow find a way back," Mark blurted out.

"I don't either," Cole agreed.

Catherine turned to face the three others. "Let's go then."

The four of them started down the dirt road, and the great-grandmother appeared from out of the shadows again with the unconscious boy slumped in her arms.

"And again, thank you for your help," Mark muttered.

"I was carrying David," the great-grandmother pointed out.

"Have you ever heard of putting him down?"

"Not when his life is in danger."

"Great excuse," Mark scoffed.

"Thank you."

Catherine looked over at the two of them. "You can't stop arguing with her. There's no doubt about it. She really *is* your sister!"

"Great. As I said before, I *love* having two of them now."

"You should," Jordan interjected.

They approached the great-grandmother's house. Mark was about to open the door when something caught Jordan's eye. The neighbor next door had turned away from them and was heading inside her house. It was the figure of a woman, but she was completely covered—head to toe—by a black cloak. Jordan couldn't see her face or body, but for a split second, a bright light that seemed to be the reflection of the sun showed through the dark covering. It sparkled from the figure's forehead. Jordan took a few steps to try to make out the person's face, but all she saw was what was causing the sparkle. It was a large ruby that was slightly protruding from under the cloak.

"Are you coming?" Mark asked.

"Ah … yeah." Jordan turned and hurried inside.

As soon as Jordan went inside, she saw her great-grandmother place David on the couch next to the fireplace. She then turned her head toward Cole. "I'm going to heal you first. He's comfortable as long as he's out, but I'm sure you're in pain."

Cole looked down at his arms. "I'm fine, really. Help the boy."

"Nonsense. Come here right now!"

Cole hung his head and approached Jordan's great-grandmother. She gently grasped his wrists and turned his arms so that the burns on the bottom side of his forearms and hands were facing up. Then she closed her eyes and started taking long breaths, in and out. She opened her eyes, and the cerulean blue glow was back. The pearl-white aura quickly surrounded her and then passed through her hands and made its way to Cole's forearms. It sparkled yellow at the sites of the burns, and in a matter of seconds, the marks were gone.

The great-grandmother blinked her eyes, and the glow disappeared. "How does that feel?"

Cole twisted his forearms back and forth and then started flexing his fingers. "It's fine."

She smiled as she walked over to David on the couch. She got down on her knees and hunched over beside him. She gently stroked the young boy's hair, and the white aura and glowing eyes came back. Then she held her hand a couple of inches away from the wound caused by the back of the soldier's rifle. The vortex of white light was released from her palm and attached itself to the injured spot on the boy's forehead. Within a few seconds, the wound was gone.

The boy's eyes fluttered open, and he looked around the room. When Jordan saw his hazel-colored orbs, her legs almost gave out.

"Oh hell no!" Mark raged.

Cole pointed and stuttered, "I-is that Mark?"

"Who else would it be?" the great-grandmother coolly responded as her aura and glowing eyes faded back to normal.

# CHAPTER TEN

# Division

"*D*on't you think that would have been good information to know?" Mark demanded.

"Not really," the great-grandmother responded.

"Why the hell not?"

"Because ... would you have changed your rescue plans if you knew?"

"Maybe?"

"Or ... would it have just made you more nervous about the plan?"

He hung his head. "Maybe." The volume of his voice went down considerably.

"I would have liked to know beforehand," Catherine said, almost in a whisper.

The great-grandmother nodded and walked up to Catherine. She placed her hand on her shoulder. "I know you love Mark, no matter what lifetime he happens to be in. But believe me, this was for the best. I didn't want you to be too emotionally involved."

"Pfftt! What are you two going to do now? Those *men* weren't human! You can't run from them forever!" Mark blurted out.

"But you see," the great-grandmother smiled, "I can see through time. So they won't catch me off guard the second time around."

"How did they catch you off guard this time?" Jordan asked.

Her older counterpart sighed. "In every lifetime, Mark feels the need to protect me. Even when I'm twenty-two, and David's only five. Our mother just died of starvation, and David wanted to save the two of us from the same fate. So while I wasn't looking, he snuck out to try to get us some food."

"How does someone sneak out from a person who can see the future? Didn't you know that was going to happen?" Mark asked in an accusing manner.

"My mother just died, and I was starving too. I wasn't functioning." She sighed. "But I can assure you that I won't make the same mistake twice."

Mark turned away.

The great-grandmother placed her hand on his shoulder. "Mark, you're right. This was completely my fault. And I needed to make it right. You have always protected me. This time, I wanted to be the one to protect you."

Mark opened up his mouth but then thought to himself for a second and closed it.

"How do I get us home?" Cole interrupted.

Jordan looked at Cole. He didn't seem happy.

The great-grandmother walked over and motioned her hand toward the circular rug. "Please sit."

Cole trudged over and plopped himself onto the rug. In comparison, the great-grandmother daintily sat down beside him. Then she called out to Mark, "Please sit next to me. I want my two favorite guys to be beside me one last time before you leave."

Cole grunted, but Mark did what she asked. She held out her hands, and both boys grudgingly grabbed ahold of them. "Jordan, you still need to sit on the other side of Cole for this to work."

Jordan looked at Cole. He *definitely* wasn't happy. She hesitantly sat down beside him. He offered his hand, and she looked at it for a second before placing her hand in his.

Catherine took the last place in the circle between Mark and Jordan. They were all connected, and the great-grandmother said, "Let's begin."

The return was much quicker than when they went to the past. It seemed that Cole had become impatient with the whole thing. When Jordan opened her eyes, they were back home—with one exception. The spot in the circle where her great-grandmother had been was now empty.

But that made it easier for Cole. He dropped Jordan's hand and shot straight up and out of the room.

"Cole, wait!" Jordan screamed. She got up and ran after him, while Catherine and Mark remained seated with curious looks on their faces.

Jordan ran downstairs and saw Cole walk out the door. He didn't even have his things. She hurried so that she could catch him before he left.

Outside, she could hear his engine starting. "Cole, wait!" She saw him through the driver's side window, but he didn't turn his head when she screamed for him.

Jordan approached the red corvette and aggressively knocked on his window. He gave her a perturbed look but then rolled the window down. "What do you want?"

"I want you to talk to me."

"Why?"

"What's bothering you? You were fine with all this up until the very end. What happened?"

He started rolling his window up. "I just want to be alone."

Jordan banged on the moving window. "No you don't. Let's talk. Just the two of us."

He glared at her from the now closed window. He looked in front of him and visibly huffed. Then he waved at her to join him.

Jordan ran over to the passenger side, and Cole leaned over to open the door for her. She jumped in. "Where are we going?"

"Out."

"That answers my question?"

"You could get *out* instead."

"Fine." Jordan folded her arms in front of her. "Just drive."

Cole nodded, thrust the gear shift, and off they went.

After a few minutes of grueling silence, Cole stopped at a red light. Jordan was looking out her window, but then out of the corner of her eye, she saw Cole's head tilt up suddenly.

He seemed to be looking at the stoplight. Jordan turned her head to see what he was so interested in and noticed the string of lights starting to swing back and forth from gusts of wind that seemed to come from out of nowhere. Then she saw a shadow sweep across the moving lights. It was a perfectly sunny day, and suddenly, the gloom crept toward them. As Cole looked around, he hissed under his breath, "Oh crap."

"Hurricane?" Jordan asked.

"No." Cole threw the gear shift into park, reached over, unbuckled Jordan's seatbelt, leaned over to open her door, and threw her out of the car. She fell backwards and hit her head on the road.

*What in the hell!* She rubbed the back of her head and then saw Cole jump out of his car door and roll on the ground. He jumped up and ran over to Jordan. His arms and legs were scratched from the asphalt. Without warning, he scooped Jordan up into his arms and ran away, with all the speed that his body could muster.

*What the hell—squared!* Jordan looked over Cole's shoulder to witness what was happening to his vehicle. The whole car was being swallowed up by the shadow. Cole kept running, facing forward and away from the vehicle. He just shook his head and muttered, "Damn shame. That was a really nice car."

# CHAPTER ELEVEN

# Examination

Needless to say, losing his car didn't improve Cole's mood. He gently placed Jordan back on the ground but didn't look at her. Instead, he was looking out toward the street.

He found what he was looking for. He waved his arm, and a moment later, a taxi pulled up in front of him. He opened the back door and said to the driver, "Take her home." He reached into his pocket and brought out a wad of cash. He pulled out four twenties and handed them to the driver. "This should be enough."

"I'm not leaving," Jordan announced.

"Yes, you are."

"What if the shadow comes back? I need you."

"No you don't." Cole sighed. "I need to end this, once and for all."

"What do you mean?" Jordan asked.

Instead of an answer, Cole shoved her in the car and closed the door behind her. Then he shouted out to the driver,

"Take her home please." The driver shrugged and then pulled away from the curb.

Cole watched the yellow vehicle as it disappeared into the distance. Now the hard part began.

He waved down another taxi as it passed by and instructed the driver how to get him home. It would be a long drive, and the driver would have to drop him off at the edge of the woods. No one else had ever seen where he stayed with Megaera.

Cole walked down the long trail that led to his home. The structure was in the middle of nowhere, with no neighbors and no sign of life for miles. His home had the look of an eerie castle, made entirely of stone, and was two stories high.

He threw open the dark mahogany door and feverishly looked around. She wasn't there, so he stormed down to the basement and found Megaera in the dungeon. Megaera turned around, and her sharp black eyes were piercing as she stared him down.

Megaera purred, "What are you doing here, Cole?"

"Leave her alone."

"Whatever do you mean?"

Annoyed, Cole responded, "Why did you send me to that place? You told me they were after *us*. But that was a lie, right? The only one we need protection from is *you!*"

Megaera laughed. "Very good, Cole. It took you long enough."

"This isn't funny to me. I'm sick of your lies. I'm not going to take it anymore."

A large grin appeared on Megaera's face. "And what are you going to do about it, Cole?"

Cole croaked out, "I'm going to stop you."

"Just like your parents did?"

Cole froze. But then he squinted his eyes at Megaera. "What. Did. You. Do?"

"I found you at the orphanage. Did you really think that was just coincidence?"

Cole was hyperventilating. "And now you plan to kill the Ivanovs?"

"No. Just Jordan. That alone should destroy the rest of them."

The rage was boiling up inside of him. "You have to get through me first."

"Who do you think you are?" Megaera laughed.

"Only the boy whose parents you killed!"

"Please, Cole. Don't act so surprised. On some level, you must have already known."

Cole couldn't take it anymore. He could hardly breathe, and his whole body glowed bright white. His fiery orange eyes looked like they could singe the walls. He was shaking throughout his sturdy frame when he went to lunge at her. But seeing this, she waved her right arm in front of her. As he leapt, the shadows formed from the floor, grabbing onto his legs and bringing him down into a dark trap. It felt like quicksand. They tightened their grip on him all the way to his thighs. He tried to struggle free, but the more he struggled, the tighter their grip became.

Cole maintained his aggressive stance. His right leg was standing toward Megaera, and his left leg was standing back two feet. Fury was seething through his face, and his eyes burned toward Megaera.

He brought his right hand from behind his back, and there was a large, orange energy ball in it. The diameter of this orb was the size of his large hand, and electrical energy pulsated through it. The intensity of the orange color illuminated Cole's immediate surroundings.

He quickly threw the ball at Megaera. But she was just as quick as he was. She sent a lightning bolt through her wrist to meet the orb midway. When the two energies collided, the explosion reverberated throughout the building, shaking it to its foundation.

Megaera raised her right hand in front of her and closed her fingers tightly. As she did, the shadows grabbed Cole's arms and pinned them behind him. He then furiously shook his head and bilocated to stand right next to her. But before he could do anything else, she sent a lightning strike toward his copy, and it exploded into a brilliant yellow light.

From where Cole stood, confined by the shadows, he simultaneously felt a sharp pain in his chest. He couldn't breathe. There was a choking and gurgling sensation within him. The top half of his body collapsed under the intensity of the sudden distress that was gripping him. But the shadows kept the bottom half of him in place, forcing him to remain standing even though he no longer had the energy to do so.

He hung his head as he started coughing up blood.

Megaera walked over and grabbed him by the hair so that he would have no choice but to look at her. "How did that feel? It must really hurt to feel the pain of death yet live through it."

His vision was clouding over, so he couldn't even respond.

Megaera dropped his head, and since he couldn't hold it up, it snapped down from her release. Then she walked up the stairs and left the basement without even a backwards glance at Cole's predicament.

Cole stood there, completely helpless, for over an hour. Then a large wolf entered the room. She was shrouded in a bright orange aura, and she was the size of a small horse.

*Why didn't you call on me?* she communicated to Cole.

He tilted his head up. *I didn't want her to get you too.*

*But, Cole. I'm a spirit. She can't kill me.*

*I can't lose you.*

*But you can lose yourself?*

*Why not? Everyone around me ends up dying!*

*That's not true.*

*It isn't? Where are my parents?*

*That's completely different. Their work here on Earth was done.*

*Who decides that?*

*Not you.*

Cole turned his head away. *I don't know why I'm even discussing this with a wolf.*

*Is there anyone else around?*

Cole huffed. *Can you get me out of this already?*

*Yes, I can.* Then the bright orange light from the wolf's aura started expanding. The light grew brighter and brighter until Cole had to squint his eyes shut to protect them from the light. One by one, the shadows started burning off. In a few minutes, Cole was able to collapse to the floor. He was free of his captors.

He lifted his head up to look at his spirit guide's eyes. *What do I do now?*

*Go back to the Ivanovs.*

*Why?*

*You have unfinished business with them.*

# CHAPTER TWELVE

## A Shattered Heart

*W*hat *unfinished business is that?* Cole asked the wolf telepathically.

*Jordan.*

Cole pulled himself up into a sitting position. *I don't know how I feel about her anymore.*

*Why?*

*Her older version lied to me. She never told us we were there to save Mark.*

*Would it have mattered?*

*I'm sick of people lying to me.*

*You've been lying to her.*

Cole turned away from the wolf. Of course, she was right. But that wasn't what he wanted to hear at the moment.

The wolf circled around Cole and sat beside him. She placed her head on his right knee. *I don't blame you, Cole. No one likes to be lied to. But both of you have been keeping secrets from each other. Besides, the Jordan in this lifetime didn't lie to you. Her past life did.*

*What's the difference?*

*She's learned a lot between lifetimes. So have you. Give her a chance.*

Cole shuddered. *Then what they said about me was true?*

The wolf looked up at him and nodded her head.

Cole took his right arm and tried to push himself up to a standing position. The wolf cautioned, *I wouldn't push yourself right now.*

He cringed but struggled out, "I can do it." He was tired of the telepathic messages already.

The wolf closed her eyes. *You were always so stubborn.*

"Thank you." He was now standing but almost fell. The wolf got up so that he could hold onto her for support.

*So you know what you have to do?*

"Don't be such a nag."

*That's what mothers are for.*

"Hmm ..." He took a step and struggled a little bit. But then he took the next one. "I could really use Jordan's past-life version right now.

The wolf looked up at him. *Why?*

"She knew how to heal."

*Why don't you ask Jordan?*

Cole looked shocked. "Does she know how?"

*She's the same soul, right?*

"Um, good point." He kept walking, using the wolf as a crutch. She helped him up the stairs and out the door. But she stopped right there.

*Will you be all right?*

Cole was slightly out of breath, but he answered, "Do I have a choice?"

The wolf tilted her head. She looked concerned, but she couldn't escort him through the city. As Cole watched, the vision of the wolf disappeared into a veil of sparkling orange light.

He turned toward the trail to the open road. It would be a long, laborious walk. He thought to himself, *I'd better get started.*

It took awhile, but he made it. There were no taxis that were driving by, so he walked to the nearest bus stop. It was about a mile in the opposite direction, but he didn't have any other option. Then it took about fifteen minutes for the first bus to come by.

Luckily, that bus dropped him off in the middle of town. From there, he was able to catch a taxi.

During the half-hour drive, he caught glimpses of his parents in his mind's eye. He had worked so hard to suppress those memories up until now, finding it too painful to think about his life before Megaera entered into it. But now, he found himself struggling to regain all the different pieces of his past.

His mother was tall and slender, with long, blonde hair. She was fair like Jordan, but her blonde hair was ash blonde, whereas Jordan's was more strawberry blonde. His mom had blue eyes as well, but they weren't quite the crystal blue orbs that Jordan's eyes were. Nevertheless, the more he thought about it, there was a definite resemblance between the two women. Maybe that contributed to his attraction to Jordan?

According to Cole's memories, his father was a couple of inches taller than his mom, and he had more of a stocky frame. His dad was dark with brown hair, brown eyes, and an olive complexion. As a result, Cole was tanner than his mom and Jordan, and he had darker blue eyes. Other than that, evidently his golden blond locks and the rest of his coloring came from his mother.

Besides remembering what they looked like, Cole had trouble recalling any of the events that led up to their demise. How could this be so difficult? If he was able to suppress these thoughts for so long, why was he unable to reverse this decision? Then a flash of recognition crossed his mind. He did have one memory of his mom before she died.

In his mind, Cole could see himself as a little boy, sitting on his bed in his room. He was all tucked in and waiting for his mom. She walked into the room and sat down beside him. His mom kissed him on the forehead and gave him a hug. Then in Cole's chirpy, sweet voice, he asked, "Who's here?"

His mom would answer, "Michael." What she meant was that Archangel Michael was there, protecting Cole always. Cole felt safe at night, sleeping by himself, knowing that the ultimate protector angel was by his side.

Cole would then chirp out, "Say the words."

His mother would smile down at him and say, "Michael, please watch over us as we sleep, and please protect us always. Please help us to feel your love, strength, and protection all around us. Please clear this house from all lower energies, lower entities, and earthbound spirits. Thank you, Michael, for always being here for us, to watch over us, love us, guide us, and protect us. Thank you, Michael. Goodnight."

Cole would chime in, "Goodnight, Michael!" Then Cole would smile back at his mother. "Michael makes ghosts go away."

Cole's mom would continue smiling at him while stroking his hair. Cole would turn over to his other side to fall asleep, as if already started on a beautiful dream. His mom would then take a gray teddy bear from his nightstand and gently place it in his arms before she left his room.

That memory suddenly disturbed Cole. Where in the heck was Archangel Michael when his parents were getting killed? Why didn't he step in on their behalf?

What was it with all these heavenly messengers? And ... Cole was supposed to be one of them! There was no reason for his parents to die. No reason!

Then he remembered what the wolf said. It wasn't up to him. He hung his head at the thought. Then what *was* up to him, if he couldn't even protect the ones he loved? Why send him to Earth if he couldn't even do that?

Suddenly, Cole looked out the window of the taxi. He was back. He was at the Ivanovs' house. What should he do now? He didn't have a plan. And he would have to crawl back to Jordan with his tail between his legs.

He paid the driver and slowly stepped out of the vehicle. But he was already seen.

Jordan walked out the door of her house with her arms crossed over her chest.

"You're back?" she accused.

"You don't want me back?"

Jordan huffed and turned her head away from him. "I didn't say that."

"So what *do* you want?"

"I want you to stop being such a flake!" The volume of her voice was increasing, as well as the intensity of her burning stare on him.

And then the pain in his chest got worse.

He clutched his heart. "Jordan, I need you to help me."

"Why should *I* help *you*?" But she took a good look at him. His face betrayed the agony that was going on inside of him, and she noticed the position of his tense hand over his heart.

"I think I'm dying."

Jordan stopped breathing. "Why?"

His breathing became more rampant. "Forget that. Get me inside."

Jordan quickly stepped over and positioned herself so that he could swing his arm around her shoulder and use her to balance as he walked toward the house.

"You really need to tell me what's going on."

Between breaths, he struggled out, "Later."

Since Cole was so much bigger than Jordan, it took great effort on her part to get him inside. His legs almost gave out when they finally reached the couch in the living room. He slumped down and curled into a ball, his head on the armrest. Jordan reached out and touched his forehead. He was feverish.

"Mom!" Jordan called out.

Catherine ran downstairs. "What is it? Is something wrong?" Then she noticed Cole. "Oh my God! What happened?"

"He won't tell me," Jordan said.

Cole reached out his hand to Jordan. "I told you that I needed your help."

Jordan's eyes widened. "What can I do?" She hesitantly took his hand into hers.

"You can heal me."

Jordan shook her head. "No I can't."

"Yes you can. You just need to believe," Cole assured.

Jordan looked over at her mom. Catherine said, "It can't hurt to try."

Jordan sighed and sat beside Cole. "What do I do?"

He took her hand and placed it over his heart. "Visualize me being healed."

"You're insane," Jordan said.

"I don't think I am. So try," Cole struggled out.

Jordan closed her eyes and tried to see Cole's heart. Inside her mind's eye, she could see the tears in it. The tears weren't lethal, and his heart was still beating, but she could only imagine the pain that those tears would bring. She could feel her hands getting warm, and in her mind, she imagined those tears being healed. She then opened her eyes. She saw the vortex of white light attach itself to Cole's chest, just like her great-grandmother had done to heal Catherine.

A couple of minutes later, the white light was gone, and Cole was visibly better.

He sat up, and Catherine asked, "Now, Cole, are you going to tell us what happened?"

Cole looked at her with his dark blue eyes. "She killed them."

Catherine shook her head. "Who? What are you talking about?"

"She killed them, and she's coming after us next."

Jordan was stunned, but Catherine continued her question. "Cole. Slow down. Who are you talking about?"

He looked away. "My guardian. She's after us. I tried to stop her but couldn't."

Jordan quickly stood up. That's what he meant by ending this once and for all. But then she squinted her eyes at him. "How long have you known this?"

He looked away from her. "Too long."

Catherine interjected, "Look, you two, we've all been through so much in the last few days. Let's not turn on each other right now."

Jordan folded her arms over her chest. "How can I trust him if he can't even tell the truth?"

Cole barked back, "Like I knew the truth when we saved your brother in the Ukraine?"

"That wasn't me!"

"Sure it was."

Catherine put herself between the two of them and raised her arms to separate them. "Okay. All that's in the past. Let's move forward. Cole, you said she killed them. Who did she kill?"

"My parents."

With a confused look, she asked, "When?"

"When I was five."

"And she's not in jail?" Catherine asked.

Cole raised his eyebrow at Catherine. "How do you put the psycho bitch from hell in jail?"

That comment struck Catherine speechless. So Jordan chimed in, "If she's so bad, how did you live with her?"

"Did I have a choice?"

"So she adopted you after your parents were killed?" Catherine asked.

"I'm sure it was the plan all along." Cole grunted. "I wish she would've killed me along with them. But I guess that would have been too easy."

"Easy for who?" Jordan asked.

"Easy for me," Cole answered.

"But then you wouldn't have been here, Cole," Catherine interjected.

"Who cares?"

"The universe, obviously," Catherine answered.

"I don't know if I believe in all that anymore. How could God let my parents die?"

Catherine looked over at Cole with empathetic eyes. Then she sat down beside him. "Cole, I don't have all the answers. And I'm very sorry that you had to go through this. But I still believe that there's a reason for everything."

"I don't."

She took his hand in hers. "All of us are subject to the karma that we create for ourselves."

Cole raised his eyebrow at Catherine again. "What do you mean by that?"

"Karma really is an eye for an eye, and a tooth for a tooth. Karma is absolute. No one can hide from the eyes of God, and no one can escape karmic law."

"And?" Cole asked.

"I'm saying that the good your parents did during their lifetime will not be ignored. And the evil that your guardian has perpetrated will not go unpunished."

Cole huffed. "When?"

"It's not for us to decide," Catherine said.

Cole turned his head away from Catherine. "Fine. So what do we do now? She's still coming after us."

Jordan had been listening to their exchange and decided to chime in. "We can sit here and wait … or … go after her."

# CHAPTER THIRTEEN

# Final Conflict

"**A**re you kidding?" Cole asked.

"Why would I be kidding?" Jordan shot him a dangerous look.

Cole raised his voice. "We need to leave—and now! There's no way for us to stop her."

"And why is that? We held our own against the demon soldiers," Jordan pointed out.

"But we didn't kill them. And Megaera won't ever give up."

"Is she a demon also?" Jordan inquired.

"No, but she's been alive since the time of Atlantis. She can't be killed."

"So she's a spirit?" Catherine asked.

"No, she has a physical body," Cole answered.

"Physical bodies can be destroyed," Catherine clarified.

"Not hers." Cole looked Catherine directly in the eye.

Catherine sighed. "It doesn't make sense. There must be a way to stop her."

"There isn't."

"Okay, Cole. Enough with the negativity. We need to come up with a plan," Catherine admonished.

Cole's mouth was open, as if he was going to counter again, but then Catherine turned to Jordan. "Honey, I need to know if you can see what's going to happen."

Jordan faced her mother with a scared expression. "What? What do you mean?"

"Your former self could heal and see throughout time. We know you can heal, so let's test out the other skill."

"Mom, I can't do it!"

"Yes, you can. Now relax and try to focus."

Jordan closed her eyes and tried to do as her mother said. But nothing came to her.

Cole walked over to Jordan and placed his hand on her shoulder. "I know you can do it."

At that second, her whole body shuddered, and the next thing Jordan knew, she saw herself standing in total darkness within her mind.

She looked up into the sky and saw a diamond shaped crystal above her. The crystal was slowly spinning and coming toward her. The crystal was enormous, and it illuminated the scene before her with bright light. Within the crystal were the colors of the rainbow, which radiated through each and every one of its many facets.

As Jordan marveled at its incredible beauty, the crystal suddenly exploded into a million pieces. As a gut reaction, she folded her arms around her face to protect her skin from the sharp shards headed in her direction. But it was no use. She crumpled to the ground and cried out in agony. The agony stemmed not only from the pain inflicted upon her, but also from the utter destruction of that object of beauty. As a result of the crystal's obliteration, Jordan found herself alone in the darkness once more.

Inside the vision, Jordan was dying, and she knew it. But within the darkness, she didn't care. *What is there to live for in total darkness? Why fight it?*

Jordan opened her eyes, and she was in her mother's arms.

"What happened? It looked like you were about to pass out," Catherine said.

Jordan explained her vision to her mother and Cole.

Catherine looked worried. "What I get from that is your destiny and the fate of the Crystal Children are intrinsically linked. If something happens to them, then you are destroyed by it. But if something happens to you, then there is no one to fight on their behalf."

"That's great. What do we do now?" Cole asked.

"Well, let's get Mark first. Then we can decide together," Catherine answered.

Catherine went upstairs and knocked on Mark's door. She waited a couple of seconds, but there was no answer. She tried to turn the knob, and it was locked.

Cole and Jordan had followed her and were now standing at Mark's bedroom doorway.

Catherine quickly grabbed a screwdriver from the hallway closet and used it to pop open the lock. Once the door was open, the three of them could see that Mark was not in there.

There was something sitting on Mark's bed in his place. It was the gray teddy bear from Cole's memory of his mom. He hadn't seen it since moving in with Megaera.

The realization struck him like a lightning bolt. Megaera was signaling to him that they were about to lose Mark like he lost his parents.

"Shit! We've got to go. We don't have much time!" Cole announced as he turned around and ran downstairs.

Jordan and Catherine didn't know where Cole was going, but they ran after him anyway.

Cole bolted outside the front door, but as soon as he was outside, he stopped dead in his tracks. Mark was pinned up against a tree by the shadow. He was unconscious.

Megaera was standing next to him with her arms crossed.

"Did you really think you could escape me so easily?" Megaera asked.

Cole squinted back at her. "Why? Why are you doing this?"

"To get you, of course." Megaera started approaching him.

Catherine and Jordan ran out the door and surveyed their surroundings. Megaera stood still for a second as she purred out, "Catherine, you can have your son back, as soon as I get mine."

"I'm not your son!" Cole barked out.

Catherine looked at Mark and then at Cole. After that, she looked directly at Megaera. "Then what? You'll use him to destroy us?"

A smile tugged at Megaera's lips. "That was the plan."

Catherine glared at her. "You couldn't do it on your own, could you?"

Megaera stepped back but then composed herself. "Why would I bother doing it myself?"

"You wouldn't. Because you're scared." Catherine continued staring Megaera down, but she also started walking in her direction.

Megaera raised her arm toward Catherine. Before she could lift it all the way up in front of her, Cole raised his arm and waved it toward Megaera from left to right. As he did this, a stream of fire blasted from his palm. He directed the flame so that it built a ring that encircled her. With the blaze dancing upwards, he had created a wall of fire in an effort to contain her.

Cole shouted back toward Jordan, "Free Mark. Light obliterates the shadow."

Jordan looked around and then up toward the sky. She raised her hand toward the sun and held it there as all the clouds in the sky divided and slowly disappeared. Then she motioned her hand directly toward her brother.

With the full power of the sun directed toward the tree, the shadow started to burn off and disappear. One by one, painful cries gave way to imploding forms, which were replaced by flames. After a minute passed, the individual fires disintegrated into puffs of smoke.

Jordan then went over and carried her brother out of the area. It was difficult and slower than she would have liked, because he was so much bigger than she was, but she had no choice. The circle of flames around Megaera was dangerously close to engulfing him too.

As Jordan was hobbling away and dragging her brother along with her, Megaera walked through the wall of flames with a devious smile. She was totally unscathed. She then fixed her stare on Catherine.

Megaera raised her hands and sent a lightning bolt toward Catherine. But Catherine was able to deflect the assault, thus sending the lightning back toward Megaera.

Megaera successfully dodged the lightning coming back her way, and this only increased her resolve to obliterate the woman before her. She tried to send another strike in the same direction, and Catherine stood firm with her arms in front of her.

As the lightning was sent, it was frozen halfway in between the two women. Megaera concentrated harder on sending out her attack, while Catherine struggled to maintain her deflection. As a result, the two of them became locked together and rendered immobile by each other. Megaera's negative energy and Catherine's positive energy were polar opposites, so as much as each of them tried, neither one could break free from the hold of the other.

Jordan watched as her mother's energy was slowly diminishing. This was a death match, and unfortunately, it seemed that Megaera was much more suited for this type of situation.

It was like it was in slow motion. Her mother's face paled, and her arms dropped just a fraction. But it was enough that the lightning strike hit its target. Jordan saw her mother's body crumple to the ground.

Jordan jumped up from her position of sitting next to her brother's unconscious body. She wanted to make sure her mother was still alive. She didn't get far though. Megaera's glare was piercing through her, and she felt it. Fear and the feeling of pure evil were seeping through every cell of Jordan's body. She was more than deathly afraid, and it made her freeze in her tracks.

"Hell no!" Cole yelled. He jumped in front of her before Megaera's lightning strike could hit her. His thigh was struck, and he fell to the ground.

*His thigh? Why was she aiming so low? Is she trying to kill me or just torture me?*

Cole reached out his hand to Jordan's. "It's go time."

*What does that mean?*

"Cole. Move away," Megaera warned.

Cole didn't acknowledge her. Instead, he continued to look at Jordan. "Remember what I said about the shadow. I won't let you go. If she takes you, then she takes me with you."

"Cole. Don't you dare!" Megaera's voice was rising in volume, and her eyes burned with intensity. But the pearl-white glow had already started to emanate from Cole's body, and his eyes had turned to a blazing orange.

Jordan took Cole's hand and shuddered as she felt the energy coming from him. Without her even trying, the white glow encompassed her as well. She couldn't see it, but her eyes were probably glowing cerulean blue like they had before.

A pearl-white mist started to swirl around them. As the mist picked up speed, Jordan's long blond hair whipped in the wind.

Megaera tried to send a lightning strike their way, but it just got lost in the mist.

A thunder clap sounded in the sky. A powerful white light emanated from them and reverberated throughout the yard. The heavy winds that had centered on Cole and Jordan were now blowing over the entire neighborhood.

Cole's wolf, surrounded by her orange aura, materialized next to Cole. At the same time, a cerulean blue dragon appeared next to Jordan. Jordan's dragon blew fire at Megaera's body, while the wolf let out a large roar.

Both spirits took on a massive translucent form. They were towering over their charges, and the energy from each animal spirit seemed to be feeding off the other.

The ground started to rumble as the energy and swirling wind intensified around Cole, Jordan, and their spirit guides.

*She seems to like lightning. I think I will give her a taste of her own medicine.*

With her glowing eyes, Jordan looked up toward the sky. She then pointed her arm from the sky toward Megaera, directing a lightning bolt to strike her.

Megaera didn't flinch. But the earth beneath her did. It split directly below her feet.

Megaera looked down too late. She tried to escape, but it was too fast. The chasm transformed into a black hole. Its immense surge of energy sucked her right in. Megaera's usual smug expression was replaced by a look of horror. Her eyes almost bulged right out of their sockets. She threw her arms above her head in a fruitless attempt to hold onto something to save herself. However, there was nothing to grab onto, so she disappeared into the darkness. Along with her went the tree that was almost completely incinerated and the circle of flames that was directly behind her.

As soon as Megaera was swallowed up, the earth slowly pieced itself back together. In just moments, the ground looked as if nothing had ever happened. A beautiful, rainbow-colored butterfly flew over the now empty patch of the Ivanovs' front yard.

At that point, the wind started to die down, and the swirling pearly-white mist around Cole and Jordan dissipated. Simultaneously, the dragon and wolf disappeared. As soon as the light encompassing their bodies and eyes faded back to normal, Cole and Jordan collapsed from the pressure of using their powers as intensely as they had, and they both fainted.

When Jordan came to, she looked over at Mark. He was now conscious, and he was sitting over Catherine's body.

*Oh my God! Mom!*

Jordan pulled herself up and crawled over to Catherine's side.

"She's alive," Mark said. But he still had a sad expression on his face.

Jordan put her hands together a couple of inches over Catherine's heart. She visualized the organ, and it was worse off than Cole's had been. But it was still beating.

Theia materialized. Jordan looked up at her. She didn't know what to say or even what to ask for.

"Don't worry. She'll be okay. Keep going."

Jordan nodded her head. She visualized the white vortex of light, and it appeared. The light attached itself to Catherine's chest.

Jordan could see with her mind's eye all the different areas of her heart being healed. It was a slow process. Each tear needed careful attention by Jordan's healing energy. But after a few minutes, Catherine's eyes fluttered open.

Jordan was so relieved that she threw her arms around Catherine's neck. Catherine flinched. The motion probably hurt, but she hugged Jordan back anyway.

Catherine then noticed Theia. "So you're the goddess that we keep hearing about?"

"Don't you remember me?"

"Should I?"

Theia laughed in her quiet, child-like way. "I think so."

Mark glared at Theia. "You started all this?"

Theia smiled. "No. You did."

Jordan looked over at Cole. He was still unconscious.

*His leg! Maybe he lost too much blood?*

Jordan hurried to his side and started healing Cole's thigh.

"Let me help you," Theia said.

The goddess waved her hand over Cole's face, and his eyes flew open. He noticed Jordan working on his leg, and then he looked around and saw that Mark and Catherine were okay.

Cole blinked as he tried to focus on the rest of his surroundings. "We got her, didn't we?"

Theia nodded. "Yes. She's finally gone."

He shook his head. "I can't believe it. I've wanted to be rid of her for so long."

"Now your life can begin," Catherine assured him.

Cole nodded, but then he looked over at Jordan. "I always believed that there was something better out there for me, but I never knew what that was."

"Did you find it?" Jordan asked, as she finished healing his leg.

"I think I did." Cole gave Jordan a sincere smile, the first one she had seen from him in a while.

Jordan glanced up at Theia. "So that was Mael, huh?"

Theia laughed. "So, did you like him?"

"I couldn't have done it without him."

"Sure you could. He just made it easier." Theia smiled. "It's nice to have friends, isn't it?"

Theia turned toward Cole. "Selene seems to help you too, right?"

"Selene?"

"Your wolf."

"She never told me her name."

"Did you ever ask?" Theia smiled.

Cole looked down at his hands. "I guess not."

"Anyway, I'll leave you all to it. I just wanted to check up on everyone."

"We'll have to move after this," Mark grunted.

"And what happened to that tree?" Catherine pointed in the direction of where the tree used to stand.

Theia looked over her shoulder. "It went with Megaera." Then she dematerialized.

# Chapter Fourteen

## Atlantis

$\mathcal{T}$he next morning, Catherine was the first one to wake up. It was extremely difficult to shake off the previous day's events. She couldn't sleep and therefore wanted to find some peace in her mind. Before dawn, she walked out to the place where they faced off against Megaera. She went over to stand at the very spot where Megaera had disappeared. Once Catherine reached her destination, it felt like an electrical jolt surged through her body. Catherine collapsed to the ground, and in her mind, she was pulled through a wormhole in time.

She noticed a light at the end of the tunnel and blinked her eyes a couple of times to focus her vision. She then observed a large, marble fountain in front of her, which was sitting in the middle of a coliseum. She looked around and saw her students listening to her giving a lecture. They were sitting on the lower level of the seating area in the large arena, and they were all intently staring at her, waiting for her to continue.

Catherine froze in terror. She didn't know what to say. She looked down at her hands, and they were tan and larger than the ones she was accustomed to seeing. She wiggled her fingers in front of her to see if the whole thing was real or an illusion. She then surveyed her body, and she seemed shorter and stockier than before. She glided her fingers through her hair, which was long and pulled back into a ponytail. She pulled her hair forward to have a look at it and saw that it was curly and jet black.

Based on her surroundings, Catherine got the feeling that she was back in Atlantis. She knew from her studies that Atlanteans chose to be outside as much as possible. They knew the benefits of being outdoors, both mentally and physically, and they capitalized on those benefits as much as they could. It would be logical that a teacher would conduct her class outdoors in order to give her students as much time in the sun and fresh air as possible.

Catherine turned to face her students and continued to give her lecture. The language she used was foreign to her, yet she was able to comprehend what she was saying. As she lectured, Catherine realized that her current life mirrored a past life she lived in Atlantis. She was even teaching subjects back then that were very similar to the ones that she was teaching her children in modern times.

At the end of the lecture, a young woman approached her with great urgency. She called out, "Deia, may I please have a word with you?"

Catherine, who was evidently known as Deia, nodded her head and followed the woman so that they could talk alone.

The woman nervously whispered to Deia, "Please beg your sister for her assistance on behalf of the healing temple. She used to help us all the time, but suddenly, she has totally abandoned us. The temple is in need of repair, and she has cut off our funds. If we do not get this taken care of, many sick people will go without our treatment. So, my lady, will you help us?"

Deia nodded her head and looked around. She left right away to go ask her sister.

Deia walked a little ways until she approached a large, gray stone castle. She passed through the large mahogany door toward the main passageway. As she approached the reception area, she could hear a woman's deep, confident voice.

This woman was having a disagreement with a young man. Deia did not want to interrupt, so she hid behind a pillar that was just beyond the huge room. Deia usually did not like to eavesdrop, but she was curious about this particular conversation.

She peeked around the pillar for a brief second and saw the woman. It was Megaera. She looked exactly like she did when Catherine saw her the day before. She was tall, thin, and pale. She had long, black hair that was thick and straight. She was wearing the crown with the large ruby in the center, and she was wearing the same long, form-fitting black dress.

Catherine then realized that the crown that Megaera wore signified that she was the queen. Furthermore, Deia was not only her sister, but she was her twin sister. Megaera and Deia were two sisters born at the same time, but they were total opposites. They didn't look or act alike. They both had long, thick black hair, but Megaera's was straight, and she always wore it down. Deia's was curly, and she wore hers in a ponytail that sat high up on her head, allowing the flowing black curls to fall gently down past her shoulder.

Deia looked softer than her sister in every way. Megaera's face was pale and narrow, while Deia's face was tan and round. Megaera preferred wearing long black dresses, and Deia wore short white dresses with a gold belt, which showed off her curvier figure. Megaera was tall and thin, while Deia was short and more heavily built.

Megaera was the first born twin, so she assumed the role of queen after their parents died. That was just fine by Deia. Deia preferred to teach and be with the children. Megaera ended up spending the majority of her time indoors, while Deia had the opportunity to spend most of her time enjoying the outdoors. Even though Megaera got all the power, she coveted Deia's happiness. Megaera desperately wanted to be happy too.

Deia recognized the young man that Megaera was arguing with. His name was Admenes, and Megaera had met him near a stream one day. Megaera had just left the healing temple, which had been her pet project for most of her young adult life, and was on her way back to the palace.

Admenes was sitting on the grass overlooking the water. As Megaera stared at him, she realized that she had never seen such a good-looking man in her life. She approached the young man and asked him to join her in the palace as her companion. He refused, and in return, she made him her slave.

Months went by, and Megaera thought that Admenes would break down and decide that a life with her was a better option than continuing to be her slave. She had seriously miscalculated. Admenes had fallen in love with a young slave girl while he was in captivity, and that was what he was telling Megaera when Deia walked in.

As soon as Admenes was done explaining his situation, Megaera's piercing black eyes stared back at him. She screamed in terror and inadvertently shot lightning out of her wrists. Admenes ducked in order to avoid the strike and then looked at the wall behind him. The lightning had torn a huge hole through the stone wall of the castle. He looked back at her in horror. As for Megaera, she looked as surprised as anyone at the fact that she could do that.

Megaera composed herself rather quickly. She told Admenes, "I am going to kill her. You saw what I can do when I get mad. Say good-bye to your girlfriend." With one arrogant look toward Admenes, Megaera turned and walked out of the room.

Deia had been very careful. She made sure that neither one of them noticed that she was listening to their exchange. When Admenes passed by the pillar, she grabbed him by the arm and pulled him toward her.

At the moment that Admenes came face to face with Deia, Catherine's consciousness recognized him. He had been facing Megaera during their exchange, so she didn't have a chance to see him before. Now that she could finally have a good look at him, there was no mistaking it. This was Mark in a previous lifetime.

Admenes looked similar to Mark. He had long, straight, dark brown hair and hazel eyes. He was tanner though, probably from spending the majority of his time outside. He was also a little bigger and more muscular than Mark.

Admenes was in his early twenties, and the months of being a slave had worn on his body and face, but the sparkle in his eyes had not been extinguished.

"We need to get you and your girlfriend out of here. Megaera is very good about following through on her threats. She will be swift and ruthless. With every second that ticks by, her threat is closer to becoming a reality."

Admenes looked down at Deia. "What should I do? You know that Megaera has me imprisoned here. There's no way the two of us can escape."

"I will help you. I'll send a guard to retrieve you and your girlfriend at sundown. We will meet at the healing temple, and then we'll go over the details of my plan."

Admenes started to walk away. A few feet down the hall, he stopped and turned back to face Deia. "Why would you do this for me?"

"I can't explain. All I know is that what she's doing is wrong. Someone has to stand up to her."

With a sad expression, Admenes bowed to Deia and proceeded out of the palace.

Deia watched Admenes as he left. Then she proceeded to the back exit. When she reached the doorway, she whispered to the guard that was stationed there, "Can you tell Nikomedes to meet me at the dock in half an hour?"

The guard stoically nodded, and then Deia walked out the door.

Deia proceeded straight out to the dock, which went into the ocean about a quarter of a mile. When she reached the end of it, she sat down at the edge, took off her sandals, and soaked her legs in the water. She looked out over the ocean and tried to formulate her plan in her mind.

A dolphin swam up and pointed its nose toward Deia. She patted its head and said, "Hello, dear friend." She then placed her hands at the base of its head and embraced him for a minute. She lamented, "I don't think I'm going to be able to visit you anymore. My life has gotten pretty complicated. I'm not sure which way I'm headed from here on out."

The dolphin looked at her with a glimmer of understanding in his eyes. He nodded his head and swam off as Deia took in one last glimpse of her cherished companion.

Deia hung her head in despair. She was lost in thought when she was startled by a familiar hand gently touching her shoulder. She looked up, and Nikomedes was standing over her.

Nikomedes was the queen's guard. Throughout his life, he had always been there to protect Megaera and her family. He had personally saved Megaera's life on many occasions. He had been fiercely loyal to the royal family, and as a result, he was trusted and respected throughout the kingdom.

During his time with the royal family, he had grown to fall in love with Deia. They never ended up together, but both knew how the other felt.

Nikomedes had a strong, straight nose and very sharp contrasts to all of his features. He had straight, black hair and dark brown eyes. He had a golden tan and was very muscular, as one would expect from the head of the queen's guard.

Deia stood up and looked Nikomedes in the eye. At that point, from within Deia, Catherine was able to see deep within Nikomedes's soul. He was Victor. Deia breathed, "Niko, I need your help with something."

"Anything, my lady. You know that."

Deia forced a smile. "Don't say that until I'm finished. I won't blame you if you say no."

Nikomedes shook his head. "I could never say no to you."

Deia carefully looked around as she whispered, "Do you know the slave known as Admenes?"

Nikomedes nodded.

"Well, it seems he found a girlfriend, and to my sister's dismay, it isn't her."

Nikomedes sighed. "I was afraid that was going to happen. I don't know why Megaera was so intent on forcing him to fall in love with her. That never works."

"Well, now she wants to kill the girl."

Nikomedes stepped back from Deia. "Do you really think she would do that?"

Deia's sad eyes met his. "Knowing Megaera …"

Nikomedes bowed his head and asked, "Well, what do you want me to do about it? You know I can't defy your sister."

Deia whispered, "I told Admenes that I would have someone meet him and his girlfriend at sundown and bring them to the healing temple."

"Then what?"

"I will have someone take the three of you far away from here."

"What about you?"

Deia shook her head. "I can't go. No one else here can keep Megaera in check, and she is clearly spiraling out of control."

Nikomedes grabbed her by the arms. "You can't control her! What are you thinking? You need to come too!"

Deia broke free from his grasp. "I told you, I can't. I have made my decision. Now will you please do this for me?"

"What makes you think that I will be able to get them out in the first place? Megaera has Admenes under close surveillance. You can't just casually walk him out of that place."

"I've thought about that too. You are Megaera's most trusted companion, so she would never suspect that you would do this. You are probably the only one in this kingdom that she isn't having watched right now."

"Hence, why you can't do it."

Deia nodded. "I'm probably the one she trusts the least."

Deia took a deep breath and then continued, "If anyone asks what you're doing with the two of them, just tell them that you're bringing them to Megaera at the healing temple. She used to spend a lot of time there. I believe you will get there safely. Once the three of you arrive, you will be shuttled away so that you don't end up getting caught."

Nikomedes did not look pleased. But then he sighed. "Fine. I will do it—for you." Even with his strong loyalty to Megaera, and his oath to the military of his land, he was unable to say no to Deia. He loved her too much. He knew that this meant certain exile for the rest of his life. With that in mind, he looked down and started thinking about what he needed to do next.

Deia looked up at him and put both of her hands on his cheeks. Tears started to well up in her eyes, and she couldn't stop herself from crying. From this moment forward, everything in their life would change. Deia reasoned that the sacrifice was worth it. But seeing the concern on Nikomedes's face made it all seem more real to her. There was no turning back, and every opportunity that they once had in life was now going to disappear.

Nikomedes wrapped his arms around her and pulled her toward him in a firm embrace. They held each other for a minute, but then Deia composed herself and said, "I guess we had better get going."

Nikomedes let go of her and said, "You're right. I'll see you at the healing temple."

"Yes. See you there." Deia slipped her sandals back on and walked away.

❀ ❀ ❀

At sundown, Nikomedes went down to the slave quarters on the far end of the palace. He knocked on the guard's door and shouted out, "I am here to pick up Admenes and another slave girl."

Since the guard on the other side was his subordinate, he gently asked Nikomedes, "Why is that?"

"Megaera sent me for them!" Nikomedes sternly replied.

"Okay. I'll get them right away."

Nikomedes started shifting his weight nervously from his right to his left, and back again, as he waited. He knew if Megaera found him there, he would be called out. That would endanger all four of their lives. He silently prayed to himself that the guard would bring Admenes and the girl quickly.

A minute later, the guard emerged with Admenes and a beautiful, young girl. She was petite. She looked especially small standing next to Admenes. She had long, ash blond hair and fair skin. She was skinny, due to her years of being a slave. However, she had more hope in her eyes than Admenes had.

"Shall we go?" Nikomedes barked out.

Admenes nodded in his direction, as the young girl looked at the two men with confusion on her face. Then they proceeded quickly out of the quarters and outside of the compound.

Once they were out of range of the castle, Nikomedes softened and politely asked the young girl, "What's your name?"

She flashed a warm smile. "My name is Eumelia."

Admenes faced Eumelia. "Can you give us a minute? I need to talk to him about something."

She looked curious but then agreed.

The two men walked away from Eumelia. When they were out of earshot, Admenes whispered to Nikomedes, "Thank you very much for helping us. However, I need to ask you one more favor."

"What is that?" Nikomedes grunted with an annoyed look.

"I haven't told Eumelia about this. I didn't want to upset her. I told her that you were here to help us escape slavery."

"Why would you lie? This affects us all."

"She didn't deserve this."

"Neither did I!" Nikomedes snapped back.

"Shh ... Please don't tell her." Admenes begged.

Nikomedes scowled at Admenes. But he grunted, "Fine."

The two of them returned to Eumelia, and Nikomedes commanded, "We need to hurry. This window of opportunity is extremely limited. We have to take advantage while we can."

They quickly approached the healing temple, and Deia was there waiting for them. She hugged Nikomedes and then put her hand on Admenes's shoulder. Deia looked over at the young girl at Admenes's side. Deia stood there frozen as she took it all in. Catherine's consciousness kicked in as she noticed the similarity to Jordan. Her long blonde hair did not have the strawberry tint that it had in her current lifetime, but other than that, she was exactly the same. She still had her fair features and was small in stature. Catherine looked around at the four of them standing there. Her family was all together, even though they were all the way back in Atlantis.

After a few seconds of Deia staring at her, the young girl stepped toward her and said, "Hello. I'm Eumelia. You're Deia, right?"

That shook her out of her thoughts. She responded, "Yes. You're right. I'm Deia. I'm sorry about that. I was just thinking about what we needed to do next."

"I know. This sort of thing doesn't happen every day."

She sounded a little too upbeat for the current situation, so Deia started to open her mouth. Nikomedes grasped Deia by the forearm and whispered in her ear, "She doesn't know."

Deia looked at her and then back at Nikomedes. She communicated through her eyes that she understood.

At that point, a beautiful, young woman with a cerulean blue aura walked toward them. It was Theia, minus her enormous wings.

"Are they ready?" she asked Deia.

Deia nodded.

Theia looked to her side, and Mael materialized beside her. He lowered his wings so that his back was available. At that moment, he was the approximate size of an elephant, except for the fact that his body was much more agile, more like a thoroughbred race horse. He bent down so that the people around him could climb on top of him.

Theia faced Admenes. "Get on."

He looked shocked, but he quickly did as he was told.

Deia motioned her hand toward Eumelia. "Let me help you up."

Eumelia looked down at her hand for a moment but then accepted it. Theia helped balance Eumelia from the other side of Mael as she climbed up behind Admenes.

Theia focused her attention on Nikomedes. "It's your turn."

He clearly didn't want to go. He turned to Deia. "Please come with us."

"I can't." She stood on her tiptoes to place a soft kiss on his cheek.

He looked down at the ground for a second. But then Theia warned, "You have to go now."

Having no other choice, he climbed up and sat behind Eumelia.

Theia waved her arm toward Mael, and the dragon took off. From inside Deia, Catherine ached as she watched her family fly away and disappear from her sight.

Theia assured Deia, "They'll be all right. I'll make sure of it."

"I know you will."

Deia slowly walked back toward the palace.

Meanwhile, Megaera had gone down to the slave quarters, looking for Admenes. When the guard told her he wasn't there, she almost went crazy. She then asked about his *little* girlfriend. The guard replied, "Nikomedes took them both. He said that he was taking them to you. Was there some sort of miscommunication?"

In response, she whipped herself around in a fit of rage. She wanted to knock the guard's head right off of his shoulders, but then she restrained herself at the last moment. She told him, "Summon all of my personal guards and have them meet me in the reception room in ten minutes!"

The guard nodded and left his post to gather everyone up. When all the men had assembled in front of Megaera, she called out, "Does anyone know where Nikomedes is?"

The young men looked around at one another, but no one had a response. She yelled out, "I don't want to have anyone killed over this. Someone knows something. I demand that you speak now!"

Most of the guards hunched over, especially the one that let Nikomedes take the slaves. However, one stepped forward. "I don't know where he is, but I do know that your sister asked to speak to him earlier. Maybe she knows?"

Megaera squinted her eyes as she thought about what the guard had just said. Deia had something to do with this. She was certain of it. But she couldn't expose what she was thinking about next to the men standing in front of her.

She announced, "Oh, in that case, maybe this isn't a problem. Deia probably has everything under control. I will follow up with her. That will be all." She waved her hand to signal they were dismissed, and she went up to her chamber.

When Deia got back to the palace, Megaera was waiting for her. Megaera had a smile on her face, and she never smiled.

"Oh, Deia, it has been such a long time since we spent an evening together. Why don't we have some dinner tonight? I already had the servants prepare some food for us."

Deia was shocked. "Megaera, I'm flattered that you want to spend time with me. But I'm tired and not really hungry right now."

Megaera shook her head. "I won't take no for an answer, dear sister. Go sit down at the table."

Through her confusion, Deia did not say no. In addition, she didn't want to appear any guiltier than she probably already did.

Megaera personally served Deia, which again was very strange. They had servants for that. Megaera brought her a bowl of soup and a glass of wine.

Deia was not very hungry, so she didn't even touch the soup. She looked over at Megaera, who had nothing to say, and Deia got even more nervous. As a response, she started to anxiously sip her wine. She couldn't tell if Megaera knew or not, but if she did, Deia would have preferred to hear her punishment straight away. The waiting was even more painful than the actual retribution would be.

After an hour of unbearable silence, Deia clutched her heart. Inside was stabbing pain, and she could hardly breathe through the agony. Her face turned bright red as she slumped over and fell to the ground. She looked up and saw Megaera smirking down at her.

Megaera purred, "Oh, Deia dear, the one who betrayed me." Megaera's eyes were flushed with the satisfaction of accomplishing her vengeance. Megaera had personally poisoned both the soup and the wine, ensuring that Deia would die if she touched either one.

Deia could no longer breathe, so she simply let go and closed her eyes. When she opened her eyes again, Catherine found herself back on the ground where Megaera had disappeared the day before. She reasoned with herself that Megaera's energy must still be present in some form, so she quickly got up and walked away.

As Catherine entered her house, she tried to make sense of everything she had just experienced. For one, even though Megaera got her revenge on Deia, she never got over the pain of losing Admenes and the betrayal of Deia and Nikomedes. This one event took a self-absorbed person and set her off on a path of evil, and an eternal life in order to escape God's judgment. Deia was satisfied in her attempt to save Admenes and Eumelia, but in return, it ended her life. She had sacrificed herself to ensure the safety of the others.

Catherine also realized after this vision that the souls of her family would find each other, time and time again, no matter what. Also, by defeating Megaera in this lifetime, Catherine finally balanced the karma of Megaera killing her during their lifetime in Atlantis.

It was probably Megaera's greatest desire to finally kill Jordan, since she had been deprived of doing so back then. And ironically, Jordan was the last one on her list. Catherine had been taken out in Atlantis, Mark was targeted in Ukraine, and killing Jordan was the final blow that was intended to take place during this lifetime.

The problem was … Megaera waited too long. Jordan had developed over the centuries, and now she was too strong for Megaera to take out on her own. Megaera counted on Cole, but she seriously miscalculated once again.

At the same time, Catherine, Mark, and Jordan had probably agreed to come back together in this lifetime to take out Megaera. Her evil reign had lasted long enough. Since they were the ones that set her off on this path, it was their responsibility to bring it to an end.

# Chapter Fifteen

## Back to the Beginning

*A*fter Catherine's experience that morning, she pretty much kept to herself for the rest of the day. But there was a bigger concern that demanded her attention. Cole was now orphaned for the second time in his life, and they had to decide what to do with him.

Catherine asked Cole if he wanted to go home to the place that he had shared with Megaera. He told her he didn't. That place held too many unpleasant memories for him to ever want to go back there. Catherine told him that she would talk it over with Victor when he got back home.

And Victor got home that night.

Needless to say, he was quite surprised to see a large, blond teenage boy occupying the guest room of his house.

He tried to vehemently object, but everyone came to Cole's defense, including Mark. Mark still didn't like the guy, but it was undeniable that Cole belonged.

Dinner was incredibly uncomfortable. Catherine sat down for this one and positioned herself right in front of Victor at the round table. Mark sat between her and Victor, and Jordan sat to her left. Cole was seated between Jordan and Victor.

Cole looked like he wanted to be anywhere but at that table.

Catherine glared at Victor. "I met your Grandmother Ivanov."

First, he looked shocked. But then he composed himself. "That doesn't really surprise me."

That infuriated her. "Um … that should surprise you. She's dead after all!"

"I know."

"So why didn't you tell us about all this?"

"I thought she was a crazy old lady."

Catherine looked like she wanted to pound the table. "But yet, you gave Jordan the amulet just like she told you to!"

"That was her dying wish. What was I supposed to do?" Victor stood up to leave the table, but then Catherine stood up too.

"But why? She said you knew everything. Why would you hide this from us?"

"Because I didn't want to lose you. Do you really think you would have married me if I told you the truth?"

Catherine thought about it and sat back down. "Maybe I wouldn't have," she said in a volume slightly higher than a whisper.

Victor huffed and sat back down himself. "I was with her the night she died."

Everyone at the table looked at him after he said that.

"She died in her sleep when I was five years old. My parents and I were visiting, and I slept with her in her bed that night. When I woke up the next morning, I tried to wake her. But she didn't move."

Victor looked down at his hands as he continued, "I couldn't understand what happened. I finally got my parents, and they found her unresponsive. They had to explain to me that she was gone."

Catherine reached over to place her hand on his. "I'm so sorry."

Victor looked her in the eye. "How could I not try to grant her last wish? Do you know what she went through during her lifetime?"

Catherine nodded. She had seen it firsthand.

"My grandmother didn't prepare me for this one." Victor glared at Cole.

Catherine smiled. "She should have. She knew all about him."

"So what's the story?"

"He's here for Jordan," Mark interjected.

And ... that was a father's worst nightmare.

Victor looked over at Catherine. "So letting him live with us seemed like a good idea?"

Catherine started fiddling her fingers. "It did at the time."

Victor faced Cole. "If you touch my daughter, I'll kill you. I don't care what kind of super powers you have. It wouldn't faze me in the slightest."

And Mark said, "I'll freeze him so that he doesn't fight back."

Then Jordan stood up. "Doesn't anyone think I can defend myself?"

"No!" Her father and brother said in unison.

"Well, that's just great. I'm supposed to lead and protect an army of Crystal Children, but I can't defend myself against a single teenage boy?"

Mark glared at her. "He was a Roman god. He's hardly a normal teenage boy."

"And I'm hardly a normal teenage girl!"

"Can I say something?" Cole asked.

"Are you still here?" Mark growled.

Cole cleared his throat and turned to face Victor. "Sir, I would never disrespect you in your own home."

"Don't disrespect me *anywhere!*" Victor warned.

"Understood."

"What about me? Can I disrespect you and attack Cole?"

Four sets of eyes glared at Jordan, who was the only one standing.

"Try not to," Catherine advised.

Jordan sat back down, and no one said anything after that. The family finished dinner, and most of them went upstairs to bed, while Catherine cleaned the dishes and table afterwards.

The next morning, Catherine sent Cole to get the rest of his things.

That gave Mark a chance to torture Jordan. "Don't think that I will let up on Cole now."

"You had better knock it off. I could make it rain on your parade every day of your life."

Mark grinned at his little sister. "That's true. But I could freeze Cole every day of *your* life. Imagine how much fun that would be."

She glared at him. "Mom!"

A few seconds later, Catherine walked in. She noticed her children staring each other down and asked, "What are you two up to?"

Jordan pointed at Mark. "He's picking on me."

Mark gave his mom a feigned innocent expression. "Me? Come on. Give me a break."

Jordan shifted her stance toward her mom. "Well actually, he *threatened* Cole."

Catherine spun around toward Mark, but before she could say a word, he retreated. "Fine. I won't bother your precious boyfriend … much." Mark left the kitchen before anyone else could say anything.

Catherine shook her head. "Don't worry about it, Jordan. I think Cole can take care of himself."

"Not if Mark freezes him first!"

Catherine looked Jordan directly in the eye. "I don't think that Cole would stay frozen for long. Then Mark would be in real trouble."

Jordan laughed. "You're probably right."

Catherine went up and hugged her daughter. "I know I am." She smiled at Jordan and walked away.

Late in the afternoon, Cole returned to the Ivanovs' house. When Jordan heard the door, she rushed out of her room to see him. Once she confirmed it was him, she ran down the stairs to greet him.

She had almost made it when Mark came into sight. He just stood there and glared at the two of them.

Cole raised his hand and did a slight wave. "Hello, Jordan."

*Well ... that's anticlimactic.*

Mark chuckled to himself and walked back into the living room.

Cole started up the stairs to put his things away. Jordan followed him.

When they reached his room, Jordan asked, "I know that you are staying with us for now, but then what are you going to do?"

Cole looked at her as he dropped his stuff. "Well, I turn eighteen in a month. At that point, I will get a place of my own. I want to enroll in college next year."

"How are you going to pay for that?"

Cole kneeled down to put his bag in the closet. In response to her question, he just silently looked up into her eyes.

She waited a few seconds but then looked down with an exasperated expression.

"Well?"

Cole sighed. "I know where Megaera's money is. The problem is that I can't get access to it until I turn eighteen."

"How can you access her money? Even if you're her beneficiary, it isn't like you can provide a death certificate for her."

Cole rolled his eyes. "And it wasn't as if she could provide a birth certificate or a driver's license in order to open an account. Don't be silly. She had a Swiss bank account that was only identified by a number—not a name. I know the number. I just have to be of legal age to transfer it to the States under my name."

"I see. Well, how much money did she have?"

"Enough."

"So you should be set for the rest of your life?"

"You could say that."

"Hmm." Jordan started paying attention to Cole's stuff that he had brought from home. For a rich man, his belongings weren't that extravagant.

He looked up at Jordan. "The money was never a big deal to me. I never got to spend it. I only got the car when Megaera sent me to your house."

He took a deep breath and said, "I loved that car. It gave me so much freedom."

"Well, in a month, maybe you could buy a new one?"

"That would be nice. But … there isn't really anything that I'm escaping from anymore." Cole turned away and continued unpacking.

After a few minutes, Cole stood up and said, "I'm done here. Do you want to go outside?"

"Sure. But for what?"

"I just like it outside. I don't like to be cooped up indoors."

Jordan shrugged. "Fine by me." Then she followed him down the stairs and out the door.

They went out to the backyard and walked up to the old tree in the right corner of the lot. It provided shade from the setting sun. Cole sat down underneath of it. Then he motioned for Jordan to sit beside him.

Cole gazed at Jordan with a serious expression. "So, tell me more about these Crystal Children. Megaera never explained it to me."

She didn't know what to say. She looked down at her hands as she answered, "They're incarnated angels. And I'm supposed to be the one that leads and protects them. That's about all I know."

Cole turned his head and faced the sunset. "And I'm supposed to help you."

Jordan looked up and hesitantly nodded. "It seems that way."

"Mmhmm," Cole said as he rubbed his eyes. Jordan couldn't tell if he was tired or if he was developing a headache.

"Have you ever seen a Crystal Child?" Cole asked.

"Not to my knowledge. But then again, Mark was supposed to be a Crystal Scout in Ukraine. And I didn't see him exhibit any supernatural powers."

"That doesn't mean he didn't have any," Cole advised.

"So maybe we've come across some Crystal Children and didn't even know it?"

"That makes sense." Cole looked toward the sunset. "No one would know about you or me just by looking at us."

"I guess you're right." Jordan sighed. "So how do we find these Crystal Children if we can't even recognize them?"

"You're the leader. You tell me." Cole gave her an impish grin.

Jordan blushed. "Well, knowing how things have been going, I'm sure they'll find me."

Cole nodded. "I did."

Jordan giggled. "Speaking of which, I want to get to know you again. I felt kind of jealous that my great-grandmother seemed to know you quite well."

"Oh yeah?" He smiled for a second, but then he pressed his lips into a straight line, and his eyes darkened. "Are you sure you don't need protection from me?"

Jordan gave him a confused look. "Why would you say that?"

"I've never been good for anyone. Not even Megaera."

Jordan scooted over so that she could look directly at him. "Megaera destroyed your life. We did what we had to do."

Cole shook his head. "And before her? I was the reason she killed my parents." He reached over and took Jordan's hands into his. "Don't you understand? I don't want you to get hurt too."

Jordan could see the pain in his eyes, and she wanted to be able to make it go away. But she realized it wasn't that simple. So as she gazed directly at him, a tear welled up in the corner of her right eye.

"No! Please no. I can't watch you cry."

Jordan shook her head and tried to hide her face. "I want to make this work."

Cole leaned over and gave her a hug. "I meant what I said. I won't let you go. We're in this together." Then he grasped her shoulders and pulled away so that he could look at her face. "But, Jordan, you have to realize something about me. I've lost so much in my life. I don't think I could handle losing someone else I care about."

Jordan started to sniffle. "I'm not planning on going anywhere."

"What if you don't have a choice?" Cole sternly asked.

She flinched but answered, "I don't believe that's my destiny."

Cole huffed. But then he reached out to her again. "Come here."

He stretched out his legs in front of him and pulled her body toward his. He wrapped his arms around her waist and firmly embraced her. He leaned his head against her shoulder, and his breath tickled her ear. "You are my twin flame."

That caught Jordan off guard, and she choked out, "What's a twin flame?"

"Two halves of one whole."

"Like a soul mate?"

"Much more." Cole gave her a hooded look.

"That's a lot to take in." Jordan had stopped sniffling and was back to her normal self. She turned away from him, but he kept his arms around her.

"It sure is."

Jordan leaned back into Cole's muscular chest. He tilted his head and whispered in her ear. "How does this feel?"

Jordan looked around to face him. "How does what feel?"

"This." And he dipped down and captured her lips in a soft, warm kiss.

Jordan was shocked. It was her first kiss, and it was with Cole. It only lasted a matter of seconds, but it was enough to take her breath away. She was glad she was sitting, or else she might have lost her balance.

Cole smiled and nuzzled his head against her shoulder. "That was nice. I could get used to this." His nose grazed her ear, and it sent a tingle down her spine.

"Are you trying to get fresh with me, Mr. Morgan?"

Cole crinkled his face. "Mr. Morgan?"

"Yep, Mr. Morgan. I'd better keep you at a distance, or my brother and father will kick your ass."

Cole laughed. "It was just a kiss. I think they can handle it."

Jordan smiled as she looked out toward the sunset. The sky was full of colorful hues, and the sight of it gave her so much hope and promise.

She had a destiny that she hadn't been counting on. But she wasn't alone. Cole would be with her, and so would her mother and Mark.

The Crystal Children's mission was to bring peace and love to Earth. But even before that, Jordan realized that love always comes around, even when it comes in the most unexpected ways. Cole was a perfect example of that. He found a way back to her, lifetime after lifetime.

At that moment, a shooting star darted across the sky. Jordan pointed at it and said, "Did you see that?"

Cole whispered in her ear, "Yes, I did. It's a good sign. I don't ignore those." He gently kissed her ear and hugged her tighter as the two of them watched the sky grow darker. The stars were becoming more visible, and it demonstrated the infinite possibilities that were available to them. Forever is a long time, but it goes by quickly when you're with the ones you love.